영어로 읽는 세계 명작
Spring Series

KB185970

The Life of Our Lord

51 주 예수의 생애

Grade
5
1400 Words

YBM Si-sa

Christianity teaches us to do good always, even to those who hurt us. Christianity tells us to love our neighbors as ourselves and to do to others what we would like them to do to us. It is Christian to be tolerant, docile, clement and self-effacing, never boasting about our virtue to others. It is Christian to show that we love God by being unassuming and by trying to do what is right at all times and in all circumstances.

YBM 사사 영어사에서는 '영어로 읽는 세계 명작 스프링 시리즈 30선'에 이어 '스프링 시리즈 추가 30선'을 개발하게 되어 '세계 명작 스프링 시리즈 60선'을 갖추게 되었습니다.

'세계 명작 스프링 시리즈 60선'은 세계적으로 가장 많이 읽히는 세계 명작 베스트 셀러만을 선정해 난이도를 6단계로 구분하여 중고생들이 영어 습득 정도에 따라 알맞은 작품을 선택하여 읽을 수 있도록 한 학습 문고 시리즈입니다.

'세계 명작 스프링 시리즈 60선'은 영어를 모국어로 하는 원어민 전문 작가 수십 명에 의해 쓰여진 것으로, 깔끔하고 유려한 필치, 자연스러운 영어 표현 등이 돋보이는 작품으로, 읽는 이로 하여금 문학적 정서에 흠뻑 빠져들게 합니다. 또한 단어, 문법, 독해를 동시에 만족시킬 수 있는 자세한 단어·구문 해설, 내용의 이해를 묻는 Quiz, Chapter별 Comprehension Checkup, Word List 등을 실어 이야기를 읽는 재미 외에 논리적이고 창의적인 보조 학습이 가능하게 합니다. 뿐만 아니라 내용의 이해를 돕는 풍부한 상황 그림, 체재의 시각적 세련미는 독자들에게 읽는 재미를 더해 줍니다.

'세계 명작 스프링 시리즈 60선'이 여러분의 영어 능력 향상에 도움이 되기를 바랍니다.

YBM)Si-sa 학습문고부

Charles Dickens는 1812년 영국 남해안 Portsmouth에서 태어났다. 아버지의 방탕하고 분에 넘치는 생활로 그의 가족들은 항상 빚에 쪼들리며 살았다. 그의 나이 열살 때 빚을 갚지 못해 아버지가 투옥되자 생활은 더욱 비참해졌다. 초등교육만 간신히 받은 채, 그는 공장에서 고된 노동을 하며 어린 시절을 보내야 했다. 이런 어린시절의 고생은 훗날 David Copperfield를 쓰게 되는 계기를 마련해 주었다.

15세 때에는 변호사 사무실의 서기가 되어 여러 가지 재판을 구경할 수 있게 되었다. 이때 접한 각양각색의 재판 광경은, 후에 A Tale of Two Cities에서 재판의 모습을 놀라우리 만치 사실적으로 묘사할 수 있는 능력의 토대가 되었다. 이 무렵 그는 스스로 속기술을 익혀 의회 출입기자가 되었으며, 틈틈이 여러 곳을 여행하며 견문을 넓혔다.

1836년에 그는 신문사에서 했던 일을 토대로 Sketches by Boz를 출판하면서 작가의 길로 들어서게 되었다. 이어 1838년에 Oliver Twist를 발표하여 선풍적인 인기를 누리면서 작가로서의 위치를 견고히 했다. 그는 1870년 59세를 일기로 세상을 떠날 때까지, Christmas Carol(1843), Hard Times(1854), Great Expectation(1861) 등등의 많은 작품을 발표했다.

Dickens는 오락적이거나 즉흥적인 작가가 아니라, 인간 삶의 모습을 사회적인 상황과 관련시켜 진지하게 추구한 Moralist라고 할 수 있다. 그의 작품들 속에는 그가 경험했던 밑바닥 생활의 적나라한 모습들이 잘 묘사되어 있으며, 그만의 유머 감각도 잘 스며들어 있다.

여기 소개되는 The Life of Our Lord는 1849년 그가 38세 되던 때 자신의 아이들을 위해 남긴 사랑의 기록이라고 할 수 있다. 여기서는 편의상 Dear readers로 바꾸었지만 원래는 Dickens가 자녀들에게 다정하게 이야기를 들려주는 형식의 소박하고 간결한 문장의 작품으로 전 11장으로 구성되었는데, 신약성서의 복음들을 기초로 해서 예수의 생애를 평이하면서도 충실하게 기록되어 있다. 이 책에서 우리는 Dickens의 자녀사랑을 엿볼 수 있으며, 예수와 기독교에 대해 좀더 알게 되는 기회를 갖게 될 것이다.

Contents

Chapter One

Dear readers, I feel it is essential for you to know something about the life of Jesus Christ. Actually, everybody ought to know and adore him. There has never been another person as altruistic, benevolent
5 or genial as he was. And no one ever showed more compassion for sinners, for the destitute, for the grieving or for those who were ill or suffering in any way. Now, he is in heaven, where we all hope to go after we die so that we can enjoy eternal beatitude
10 with God. You can never conceive of what a splendid place heaven is without knowing who Jesus was and everything that he accomplished.

adore 숭배하다, 찬미하다
altruistic 이타적인
benevolent 자비로운, 인정 많은
genial 다정한, 친절한
compassion 동정, 불쌍히 여김
sinner 죄인
destitute 빈곤한

grieve 몹시 슬퍼하다
so that …하도록
eternal 영원한
beatitude [bi(:)ǽtit(j)ùːd]
　　더할 나위 없는 행복
conceive of 상상하다, 마음에 그리다
splendid 멋진, 근사한

· ·

3 There has never been another person as altruistic, benevolent
or genial as he was.
그 분만큼 이타적이고 자비롭고, 다정한 사람은 결코 없었습니다.

5 no one ever showed more compassion for sinners, for the
destitute, for the grieving or for those who were ill or suffering
in any way
죄인들, 궁핍한 자들, 슬퍼하는 자들, 병들고 여러 면에서 고통받는 사람들을
그 보다 더 불쌍히 여긴 사람은 여태껏 아무도 없었습니다.

8 heaven, where we all hope to go after we die so that we can
enjoy eternal beatitude with God
천국, 그 곳은 하나님과 더불어 영원한 축복을 누리기 위해, 우리 모두가 죽은
후에 가고 싶어하는 그런 곳이죠.

10 You can never conceive of what a splendid place heaven is
without knowing who Jesus was and everything that he
accomplished.
예수가 누구인지 그리고 그분이 이룩한 모든 행적을
알지 못하고서는 천국이 얼마나 멋진 곳인지
여러분들은 결코 상상할 수 없을 것입니다.

What is the speaker's
attitude toward Jesus?

① respectful
② critical
③ mocking

9

ANS. 1

He was born about two thousand years ago in the country of Israel in a town called Bethlehem, the birthplace of King David. However, he grew up in a northern city of Israel called Nazareth. His earthly father's name was Joseph and he was a carpenter. His mother's name was Mary and she was the most exalted of all women because she was the mother of God. Prior to Jesus's birth, his mother and father had to make a long journey to Bethlehem to participate in a national census because Joseph was of the lineage of King David's house.

When they arrived, the town was teeming with people who were also there to be counted in the census. Joseph and Mary couldn't find any lodging and were forced to sleep in a barn, which is a place where farm animals are housed and fed. This humble shelter is where Jesus Christ was born. Now

there was no bed or any kind of luxury in the barn, so Mary had to lay her newborn baby in a manger. A manger is a trough or a large box that contains feed for livestock. He was satisfied with his less-than-adequate makeshift crib and soon fell into a deep slumber.

earthly 이 세상의, 현세의	manger[méidʒər] 여물통, 구유
exalted 고귀한, 숭고한	trough[trɔːf] 여물통, 구유
prior to …이전에	feed 여물
national census 국가의 인구조사	livestock 가축
lineage (보통 명문가의) 혈통, 계통	less-than-adequate 불충분한, 부적당한
teem with …이 충만하다, 많다	
lodging 숙박	makeshift 임시 변통물, 미봉책
house …에 거처할 곳을 주다, 수용하다	crib (소아용) 침대
	slumber 잠

· ·

10 Joseph was of the lineage of King David's house
요셉은 다윗 왕의 혈통이었다.

12 the town was teeming with people who were also there to be counted in the census
마을은 인구조사를 받기 위해 온 사람들로 북새통이었다.

He was satisfied with his less-than-adequate makeshift crib 그 분은 아기에게 부적당한 임시 방편으로 마련된 침대에 만족하시고

아기 예수의 출생지는?

① Jerusalem
② Bethlehem
③ Nazareth

While he was sleeping, some shepherds were tending their flocks in a field nearby. Suddenly, they saw a celestial being, an angel of God descending from heaven towards them. At first, they were 5 afraid and fell prostrate on the ground, hiding their faces. But the angel said, "Do not fear! I bring news of great joy! Today, there was a child born in Bethlehem who is the Son of God. He will grow up to be a great man and God will use him to ransom 10 his people. He will show everyone how to love and how to find genuine peace and fulfillment. His name will be Jesus Christ, and everyone will invoke his name in their prayers because it is sacred and because God loves it." Then the angel told the 15 shepherds to go to the barn where they would find the infant Jesus lying in a manger. They did as they were instructed and found everything just as the 20 angel had said. They all proclaimed together, "God bless this child!"

shepherd 양치기, 목동	ransom 몸값을 받고 석방하다,
tend 돌보다	속죄하다
flock (동물의) 무리, 떼	genuine 진정한
nearby 근방의, 근처의	fulfillment 성취, 달성
celestial[silést∫əl] 천상의, 하늘의	invoke 기원하다, 빌다
being 존재	sacred 신성한, 거룩한
descend 내려오다	infant 유아
(반의어는 ascend)	instruct 지시하다
prostrate 엎드리다, 엎드린	proclaim 찬양하다

．．．．．．．．．．．．．．．．．．．．．．．．．．．

5 (they) fell prostrate on the ground, hiding their faces
(그들은) 얼굴을 가린 채로 땅에 엎드렸다.

10 He will show everyone how to love and how to find genuine
peace and fulfillment. 그 분은 어떻게 사랑하고, 어떻게 진정한 평화와
성취를 발견할 수 있는지를 모든 이들에게 보여줄 것이다.

17 They did as they were instructed and found everything just as the
angel had said. 그들은 지시 받은 대로 행하였더니, 바로 천사가 말했던 그
모든 것들을 찾을 수 있었다.

목동들이 아기 예수를 발견한
장소는?

① 여관
② 성전
③ 마구간

The greatest place in all of Israel was a southern city called Jerusalem. In Jerusalem, there lived a king whose name was Herod. One day, some astrologers came from a country in the Far East and

5 said to the King, "We have seen a great star in the sky which signifies the birth of a king. He will grow to be a man who is loved and esteemed by everyone."

When King Herod heard this he was extremely

10 jealous because he was a malicious, depraved man. In front of the wise men he pretended to be gracious and said, "Where is this newborn king?"

The wise men answered, "We are uncertain, but if we continue to follow the star, it will show us. It

15 had been guiding us as we traveled here, but now it is standing still in the sky." Herod asked them to inform him of the child's whereabouts as soon as they found him. Then they left Jerusalem and the star began moving again just ahead of them. Finally,

20 it stopped right over the place where baby Jesus lay.

Jerusalem 예루살렘
Herod 헤롯(로마의 왕 중 하나)
astrologer [əstálədʒər] 점성가
signify 알리다, 나타내다
esteem 존경하다

malicious 사악한
depraved 타락한, 사악한
gracious 호의적인, 친절한
whereabouts 거처
ahead of …에 앞서

· ·

6 He will grow to be a man who is loved and esteemed by
everyone. 그는 자라서 모든 이들의 사랑과 존경을 받는 사람이 될 것입니다.

14 It had been guiding us as we traveled here, but now it is
standing still in the sky. 우리가 여기까지 여행하는 동안 그 별이
줄곧 우리를 안내해 주었는데, 지금은 그 별이 하늘에 멈춰 있습니다.

16 Herod asked them to inform him of the child's
whereabouts as soon as they found him.
헤롯은 그들이 아기를 찾자마자 그의 거처를
알려달라고 요청했다.

20 it stopped right over the place
where baby Jesus lay
그 별은 아기 예수가
누워있는 장소 바로
위에서 멈춰 섰다.

본문에서 Herod의 성품을
묘사하는 말이 아닌 것은?

① gracious
② jealous
③ malicious

5

The astrologers went inside and saw the child with Mary, his mother. A sense of wonder filled their hearts and they knelt in adoration. Then they presented him with some extraordinary gifts: gold
5 for a king, incense for God and myrrh for death. Later, as they were preparing to leave for their own country, an angel told them in a vision to return by a different route than they had come because Herod wanted to kill the child. So, they had to travel
10 secretly by night for fear that Herod would force them to reveal where Jesus was.

Approximately one month later, another angel appeared to Joseph and bid him take Mary and the child to a distant country called Egypt. They had to
15 escape because Herod planned to slaughter every baby boy in Bethlehem under two years old. Even

though the journey was long and perilous, they arrived in Egypt unharmed and stayed there for several years.

---

majesty 위엄, 장엄
kneel 무릎을 꿇다
　　　(kneel-knelt-knelt)
adoration 존경, 경배, 숭배
extraordinary 진귀한
incense 향(유향)
myrrh [mə́:ri] 몰약
vision 환상

reveal 밝히다, 드러내다
approximately 약 , 대략
bid 명령하다
　　(bade or bad- bidden or bid)
slaughter 살해하다
perilous 위험한
Egypt 이집트(애굽)
unharmed 해를 입지 않은

· ·

2 A sense of wonder and majesty filled their hearts
마음은 경이로움과 위엄으로 가득 찼다.

3 they knelt in adoration 그들은 경배하기 위해 무릎을 꿇었다.

3 they presented him with some extraordinary gifts
그들은 그에게 몇 가지 진귀한 예물을 드렸다.

7 an angel told them in a vision to return by a different
route than they had come 천사가 환상 중에 나타나
그들에게 다른 길로 돌아가라고 말했다.

10 for fear that Herod would force them to
reveal where Jesus was. 헤롯이 그들에게
예수의 거처를 밝히라고 강요할 것이 두려워

13 bid him take Mary and the child
to a distant country called
Egypt 그에게 마리아와
아기를 이집트라는 먼
나라로 데리고 가라고
명했다.

What did the astrologers
give to the child, Jesus? Fill
in the blanks in English.

They gave Jesus _____,
_____, and _____.

ANS. gold (for a king), incense (for God), myrrh (for death)

Chapter Two

After King Herod had died, an angel came again to Joseph and said that it was safe for them to return to Israel and that they need not be afraid. So, Joseph, Mary and her son Jesus, also known as the
5 Holy Family, started out for Jerusalem. On the way, they heard that King Herod's son, Herod Antipas, was now ruling over the land. They were anxious that he too might want to destroy their child, so they decided to flee to the northern part of Israel: to
10 Nazareth. It was there that they settled down and made their home.

When Jesus was about twelve years old, Joseph and Mary took him to Jerusalem to participate in the Passover, an important religious festival. There
15 was to be a huge celebration in a temple, which was like a big church or cathedral. It was the center of worship for all Jewish people at that time. After the

festival was over, they left Jerusalem for their hometown. They made the three-day journey in a caravan with many of their friends and relatives. Traveling together would prevent them from being
5 attacked by robbers, and it would make the tiresome trip less difficult.

Herod Antipas 헤롯 아켈라오
flee 도망치다
settle down 정착하다
the Passover 유월절(유대인의 명절 중 하나)
cathedral[kəkθíːdr(ə)l] 성당

worship 숭배, 예배
Jewish 유대인의
caravan (이주민의) 마차대
prevent ~ from … ~가 …하는 것을 막다
tiresome 지치는, 지루한

· ·

10 It was there that they settled down and made their home.
그들이 정착하여 가정을 이룬 곳은 바로 그곳이었다.

14 There was to be a huge celebration in a temple,
그 사원에서 큰 경축 행사가 있을 예정이었다.

16 It was the center of worship for all Jewish people at that time. 그 당시에 그곳은 모든 유대인들의 예배의 중심지였다.

4 Traveling together would prevent them from being attacked by robbers, 함께 여행하는 것은 그들에게 강도들의 공격을 막아주었다.

Joseph과 Mary가 예수님을 데리고 예루살렘으로 간 이유는?

① 예루살렘을 구경시켜주기 위해
② 유월절 행사에 참여하기 위해
③ 유대인 율법을 가르쳐주기 위해

ANS.2

For a whole day Joseph and Mary traveled on without realizing that Jesus was not with them. Even though they didn't see him, they thought he must be somewhere in the caravan. Once they
5 actually began searching for him, they discovered he wasn't there, so they went back to the city to search for him. Three days later, they finally found him sitting in the temple speaking to a group of elders about the beneficence of God and how we should
10 pray constantly. Some of the people listening to Jesus were learned men called doctors. They were not the kind of doctors, who cured sick people, but they were scholars and wise men. Jesus showed
15 such insight and wisdom by what he said to them and by the questions he asked that they were all astounded.

Mary, Jesus's mother, approached him and said, "Son, we've been so worried about you. Why did
20 you go off alone and make us search for you for three days?"

"Why were you looking for me?" Jesus asked. "Didn't you know that I would be in my Father's house?" Then he went back to Nazareth with Joseph and Mary and lived there until he was around thirty years old.

elder 원로, 연장자
beneficence [binéfis(ə)ns] 은혜
constantly 지속적으로
learned 학식 있는
scholar 학자

such ~ that… 너무나 ~해서 …하다
insight 통찰력
astound [əstáund] 놀라게 하다
approach 다가가다
go off (말없이) 떠나다, 사라지다

· ·

1 traveled on without realizing that
  …를 깨닫지도 못한 채 계속해서 여행을 했다.

4 Once they actually began searching for him,
  그들이 실제로 그를 찾기 시작했을 때

7 they finally found him sitting in the temple speaking to a group of elders 그들은 마침내 그가 원로들과 얘기를 하면서 사원에 앉아있는 것을 발견했다.

10 Some of the people listening to Jesus were learned men called doctors. 예수의 말을 경청하고 있었던 사람들 중의 일부는 박사라 불리우는 학식 있는 사람들이었다.

14 Jesus showed such insight and wisdom by what he said to them and by the questions he asked that they were all astounded. 예수는 그들에게 한 말과 질문을 통해 굉장한 통찰력과 지혜를 드러내서 그들 모두를 놀라게 했다.

Joseph과 Mary가 예수님을 발견한 장소는?

① in a caravan
② in the temple
③ in Nazareth

21

Chapter Three

Many people began following Jesus because they wanted him to teach them how to find happiness. Some men, called disciples, even gave up everything they had—jobs, families, friends—so they could
5 accompany him wherever he went. Once, he went up onto a mountain and spoke at great length to all the people gathered around him. From his own mouth, he taught them the prayer that begins, "Our Father, who is in heaven, may Your name be
10 praised," and he commanded his disciples to use those words whenever they prayed. This is the same prayer that you pray each night before going to bed. It's called The Lord's Prayer since Jesus was the first one to say it.

disciple[disáipl] 제자, 문하생   command 명령하다

accompany 수반하다, 함께 다니다   The Lord's Prayer (기독교의)

at great length 오랫동안   주기도문

. . . .

3 even gave up everything they had
그들이 가진 모든 것을 포기하기까지 했다.

4 they could accompany him wherever he went
그들은 그가 다니는 곳은 어디나 따라다닐 수 있었다.

6 (he) spoke at great length to all the people gathered around
him. 그 주위에 모여있던 모든 사람들에게 아주 오랫동안 말씀을 하셨다.

8 Our Father, who is in heaven, may Your name be praised,
하늘에 계신 우리 아버지여, 당신의 이름이 찬양 받기를 원하나이다.

10 he commanded his disciples to use those words whenever they
prayed 그는 그의 제자들에게 그들이 기도할 때마다 이 말을 사용하라고
명하셨다.

13 It's called The Lord's Prayer 그것은 주기도문이라고 불리운다.

많은 사람들이 예수님을
따라 다닌 이유는?

① to learn how to find
happiness

② to learn how to become
disciples

③ to learn how to pray

3

When he came down from the mountain, there was a man waiting to see him. The man had a dreaded skin disease called leprosy. It was common for people in those days to have leprosy, and anyone 5 who had it was called a leper. This leper came up to Jesus and fell down at his feet saying, "Lord! If you want to, you can make me well again!"

Jesus felt sorry for the leper, and so he stretched out his hand and said, "I do want to! Be healed of 10 your disease!" At once, the leprosy disappeared and the man was cured.

Eventually, Jesus became so popular that huge hordes of people surrounded him at all times. 15 One day, he and his disciples sought refuge from the crowds in a friend's house. Nevertheless, because there were so many people 20 outside who desperately wanted to see him, he had no choice but to let them in.

dreaded 끔찍한	surround 둘러싸다
disease 질병	at all times 항상
leprosy[léprəsi] 문둥병	seek 찾다
leper 문둥병자	refuge 피할 곳, 피난처
feel sorry for 불쌍히 여기다	nevertheless 그럼에도 불구하고
stretch out 뻗다	desperately 필사적으로
eventually 마침내	have no choice but to
horde 대집단, 군중	…하지 않을 수 없다

• •

6 (This leper) fell down at his feet saying,
(이 문둥병자는) 그의 발아래 엎드려 말했다.

6 If you want to, you can make me well again!
당신이 원하신다면 나를 다시 낫게 하실 수 있습니다!

7 Jesus felt sorry for the leper, 예수님은 그 문둥병자를 가엾게 여기셨다.

9 I do want to! Be healed of your disease!
내가 진심으로 원하노니 너의 병이 나을지어다!

12 so popular that huge hordes of people surrounded him at all
times 너무 인기가 많으셔서 거대한 군중들이 항상 그를 에워싸고 다녔다.

21 he had no choice but to let them in
그들을 들여보내지 않을 수 없었다.

문둥병자에 대한 예수님의 태도는?

① 책망하심
② 측은히 여기심
③ 멀리하심

25

ANS. 2

In the crowd there was a man who was sick with palsy, which made him shake all over and prevented him from standing or moving by himself. Some of his relatives carried him on a mat up to the house
5 where Jesus was, but they couldn't get inside because there were too many people. They realized they wouldn't be able to get near Jesus if they didn't find another way into the house. So, they went up onto the roof and took off some of the tiles, making
10 a hole large enough for the paralytic to fit through. Then, they fastened him to his mat and lowered him down into the house. When Jesus saw the paralytic, his heart was almost broken and he said,

"Get up! Pick up your mat and go home!"
15 Immediately, the man stood up, picked up his mat and walked away praising and thanking God.

palsy [pɔ́ːlzi] 중풍, 마비 fasten 고정시키다
take off 떼어내다 lower down 내리다
paralytic 중풍병자, 마비환자 immediately 즉시
fit through 통과하다 praise 찬양하다

· ·

7 they wouldn't be able to get near Jesus
그들은 예수님 가까이 가는 것이 불가능하였다.

9 making a hole large enough for the paralytic to fit through
중풍병자가 통과하기에 충분히 큰 구멍을 만들었다.

중풍병자가 집안에 들어온
방법을 잘 설명한 것은?

① 창문을 통해 들것에 실려 들어옴
② 다른 사람의 부축을 받으며 문으로
    들어옴
③ 천장(지붕)에서 들것에 실려 내려옴

Of all the people who came to see Jesus, there was no one as distraught as the judge. He got down on his knees and cried out, "Oh Lord! My only daughter, my beautiful, good, 5 innocent little girl, is dead! Please come and lay your hands on her and bring her back to life. Her mother and I love her 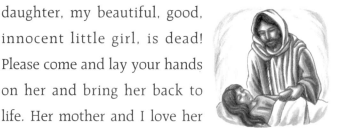 so much and we can't bear to live without her. I 10 believe you can do this!" So, Jesus and his disciples went with the judge.

When they arrived at his house, his friends and neighbors were there weeping and mourning. Jesus looked with pity at the poor little dead girl. To 15 comfort her parents he said, "She isn't really dead. She is only sleeping." Then he told everyone to leave the room and went over to where the girl was lying. He took her by the hand and she got up just as if she had only been asleep. Her parents came 20 back into the room and were so elated that they picked her up, hugged her and kissed her all over! They thanked God and Jesus for that miracle and for having mercy on their daughter.

Jesus was always merciful and tender to everyone. Because he helped so many people and taught them how to get to heaven, he was called our Savior.

---

distraught [distrɔ́ːt] 괴로운, 마음이 산란한
get down on one's knees 무릎 꿇다
innocent 순진한, 천진난만한
bear 참다, 견디다

weep 울다, 흐느끼다
mourn 통곡하다
comfort 위로하다
elated [iléitid] 기분이 고조된
mercy 자비
tender 다정다감한, 동정심이 있는

. . . .

1 there was no one as distraught as the judge
재판관만큼 마음이 괴로운 사람은 아무도 없었다.

18 He took her by the hand 그는 그녀의 손을 잡았다.

19 as if she had only been asleep 마치 그녀가 잠을 잤던 것처럼

20 so elated that they picked her up, 기분이 너무 좋아서
그녀를 번쩍 들어올렸다.

22 They thanked God and Jesus for that miracle
and for having mercy on their daughter.
그들은 하나님과 예수님께 그 기적과
딸에게 자비를 베풀어주신 것에
대해 감사했다.

재판관이 예수께 간절히 요청한 것은?

① 오셔서 가족들을 위로해 달라.
② 죽은 딸을 살려달라.
③ 병든 딸을 고쳐달라.

Chapter Four

In Israel, where our Savior performed his miracles, most of the inhabitants were Jews. Among the Jews, there were some men called Pharisees who were very proud and thought that no one was
5 superior to them. They heard about Jesus and were afraid of him because he was so popular and he taught with greater skill and authority than they did.

One Sunday, our Savior was walking in some
10 fields with his disciples. They were hungry so they picked some wheat that was growing there and ate it. The Pharisees said this was sacrilegious because they did it on Sunday, which the Jews call the Sabbath. According to Jewish law, nobody is
15 supposed to do any kind of work at all on the Sabbath.

perform 행하다	wheat 밀
inhabitant 거주자, 주민	sacrilegious [sæ̀krilíːdʒəs]
Jew 유대인	신성모독의, 벌받을
Pharisee 바리새인	the Sabbath 안식일
(종교상의 형식주의자)	according to …에 따르면
superior to …보다 우월한	Jewish 유대인의
authority 권위	be supposed to …하기로 되어 있다

....

4 no one was superior to them 아무도 그들보다 우월하진 않았다.

13 they did it on Sunday, which the Jews call the Sabbath
그들은 일요일날 그 일을 행했는데, 유대인들은 그 날을 안식일이라 불렀다.

14 According to Jewish law, nobody is supposed to do any kind of
work at all on the Sabbath. 유대인의 법에 따르면, 누구든 안식일에는
어떠한 일도 하지 않기로 되어있다.

What do the Jews call Sunday?
Fill in the blank in English.

They call it _____.

ANS: the Sabbath

The Pharisees also said it was wrong when Jesus went into a synagogue, which is similar to a church, and wanted to heal a poor man whose hand was deformed. They asked, "Is it right to cure people on 5 the Sabbath?"

Jesus answered, "If you had a sheep and it fell into a pit on a Sunday, wouldn't you try to rescue it? Isn't a human being greater than a sheep?"

Then he said to the poor man, "Stretch out your 10 hand!" When the man put out his hand, it looked normal like the other one. Jesus spoke out loud for everyone in the synagogue to hear, "It is permissible to do a good deed no matter what day of the week it is. 15 God is greater than the Sabbath."

synagogue [sínəgɔːg] 유대교 회당   rescue 구조하다, 구하다
heal 치료하다   permissible 허용할 수 있는
deform 불구로 하다   deed 행동, 행위
pit 구덩이   no matter what 무엇이든지 간에

• •

3 heal a poor man whose hand was deformed
손이 불구인 불쌍한 사람을 고치다

6 If you had a sheep and it fell into a pit on a Sunday, wouldn't you try to rescue it? 만약 당신이 양을 한 마리 가지고 있는데 그 양이 일요일 날 구덩이에 빠진다면, 당신은 그것을 구하려 하지 않겠소?

10 it looked normal like the other one
그것은 다른 쪽 손처럼 정상으로 보였다.

11 spoke out loud for everyone in the synagogue to hear
회당에 모인 사람들 모두 들을 수 있도록 큰 소리로 말씀하셨다.

13 no matter what day of the week it is
무슨 요일이든지 간에

예수께서 구덩이에 빠진 양의 비유를 드신 이유는?

① 안식일에 생명을 구하는 일은 정당하다는 것을 말씀하시고자
② 안식일의 중요성을 강조하시고자
③ 안식일의 폐지를 말씀하시고자

ANS.1

Chapter Five

Not all of the Pharisees were bad men. One Pharisee, whose name was Simon, begged our Savior to come to his house for a dinner party. While they were all reclined at the table, a woman 5 who was known to be a prostitute entered the room. At first, she felt ashamed of herself and was afraid to come near Jesus. But she heard that he showed mercy to anyone who had done wrong but who were truly contrite and wanted to amend their 10 lives. Little by little, as she listened to Jesus speak, her confidence in his goodness increased. Eventually, she came up behind the place where he was lying, dropped down at his feet and began to cry. With the flood of her tears, she washed his feet, 15 kissed them and dried them with her long hair. Then she rubbed them with some expensive, sweet-

had brought with her. The woman's name was
Mary Magdalene.

Simon 시몬	amend (행실, 잘못 따위를)
beg 간청하다	고치다, 바로잡다
recline 기대게 하다, (몸을) 눕히다	confidence 확신
(이 당시에는 비스듬히	goodness 선하심
누워서 식사를 함)	drop down 엎드리다
prostitute 창녀	rub 문지르다, 닦다
feel ashamed of	sweet-smelling
수치스러움을 느끼다	향기로운 냄새가 나는
contrite [kəntráit] 회개하는	Mary Magdalene 막달라 마리아

• •

4 While they were all reclined at table, a woman who was known
to be a prostitute entered the room. 그들 모두가 식탁에서 기대어
있었을 때, 창녀로 알려진 한 여자가 방으로 들어왔다.

10 her confidence in his goodness increased
그의 선하심에 대한 그녀의 확신이 증가되었다.

12 she came up behind the place where he was lying,
dropped down at his feet 그녀는 그가 누워있었던
곳 뒤로 다가와서 그의 발 아래 엎드렸다.

13 With the flood of her tears,
하염없이 흐르는 눈물로

여인이 보인 행동이 아닌 것은?

① 눈물을 흘렸다.
② 예수님의 발에 입을 맞췄다.
③ 멀리서 예수님을 지켜보기만 했다.

When the Pharisee who had invited our Savior to dinner saw what was happening and how he let this sinful woman touch him, he was surprised. He thought to himself, "Jesus must not know what kind of woman this is."

But Jesus could read his mind and so he said,

"Simon, if a man lent five hundred dollars to one man and fifty to another then canceled both of their debts, which man do you think would be more grateful?"

Simon answered, "I suppose the man who had borrowed more money would be more grateful."

Jesus said, "You're right! Because God has forgiven this woman who has sinned so much, she will be more thankful and love Him more." Then he turned to the woman at his feet and said, "God forgives you!" Everyone at the dinner party wondered what Jesus meant. They believed that only God had the power to forgive sins. God had given Jesus a mandate to forgive people's sins, but no one could comprehend this.

sinful 죄 많은	sin 죄짓다
cancel 취소하다	mandate [mǽndeit]
debt 빚	위임, 권한
grateful 감사하는	comprehend 이해하다

. . . .

4 Jesus must not know what kind of woman this is.
예수께서는 이 여인이 어떤 사람인지 모르시는 게 틀림없어.

7 Simon, if a man lent five hundred dollars to one man
and fifty to another then canceled both of their
debts, which man do you think would be
more grateful? 시몬아, 만약 어떤 사람이
한 사람에게는 500달러를 빌려주고 또
다른 사람에게는 50달러를 빌려준
다음, 그들 둘 다의 빚을 탕감해
준다면, 너는 어떤 사람이
더 고마움을 느낄거라
생각하느냐?

이 여인에 대한 사람들의 태도는?

① 경멸함

② 측은히 여김

③ 용기를 부러워 함

There were so many people who came to Jesus to be taught and healed of their illnesses that he hardly ever had time to rest. Once, he tried to get away from all the people by sailing out onto a lake 5 with his disciples. But the people saw this and ran ahead to the other side. When he got out of the boat on the opposite shore, there was another huge crowd waiting for him.

Jesus saw that these people were like sheep 10 without a shepherd. He had pity on them and said to Philip, one of his disciples, "They must be hungry after following me such a long distance. Where can we buy enough bread to feed all these people?"

Philip answered, "Lord, two hundred dollars 15 worth of bread wouldn't be enough to satisfy these people, and all we have are five loaves of bread and two small fish. What can we do with such a small amount of food?"

Then Jesus told everyone to sit down on the 20 grass in small groups. After they were all seated, he took the bread, looked up to heaven and handed it in pieces to his disciples, who handed it to the people. Out of those five loaves and two fish, thousands of men, women and children were fed. When they all had enough to eat, the disciples collected twelve baskets full of leftovers. This was another one of the great miracles Jesus Christ performed.

hardly ever 좀처럼 …하지 않다	satisfy 만족시키다
opposite 반대편의	loaf[louf] 덩어리
distance 거리	a small amount of 적은 양의
worth of …의 가치가 있는	leftover 남은 것, 남은 음식

· ·

1 There were so many people who came to Jesus to be taught and healed of their illnesses that he hardly ever had time to rest.
가르침을 받고 그들의 질병을 치료받기 위해 예수께 나오는 자가 너무나 많아서 그는 좀처럼 쉴 시간이 없으셨다.

21 handed it in pieces to his disciples, who handed it to the people 그것을 조각으로 나누어 제자들에게 건네주었고,
그들은 그것을 사람들에게 나눠주었다.

Out of those five loaves and two fish, thousands of men, women and children were fed. 빵 다섯 덩어리와 물고기 두 마리로 수천 명의 남자와 여자들 그리고 아이들을 먹였다.

With how much food did Jesus feed them all?
Write in English.

ANS. (Jesus fed them) With five loaves of bread and two fish.

Comprehension

Checkup I

1. 아기 예수께 찾아온 사람이 <u>아닌</u> 것은?

① shepherds   ② astrologers   ③ Herod

2. 아기 예수가 태어난 장소를 묘사하는 표현이 <u>아닌</u> 것은?

① the humble shelter

② his less-than-adequate makeshift crib

③ the place with many kinds of luxury

3. 본문을 살펴보며 아기 예수의 이동 경로를 순서대로 나열하시오.

> Nazareth, Bethlehem, Egypt
>
> _____ ➡ _____ ➡ _____

4. Joseph과 Mary가 아기 예수를 데리고 이집트로 간 이유는?

① 이스라엘에 흉년이 들어서

② Herod이 두 세 미만의 남자 아기들을 죽이려 했기 때문에

③ Joseph과 Mary의 고향이었기 때문에

5. 예루살렘에 대한 설명으로 바르지 <u>않은</u> 것은?

① 이스라엘의 중심 도시

② 유월절 축제가 열리는 곳

③ 예수의 고향

6. 관련 있는 것끼리 서로 연결하시오.

① 재판관   ⓐ 죽은 딸을 살려달라고 예수께
                                     간청함

② Mary Magdalene   ⓑ 예수님을 저녁식사에 초대함

③ Simon   ⓒ 비싼 향유로 예수님의 발을 닦음

7. 예수님이 행하신 일이 <u>아닌</u> 것은?

① 병자를 고치심
② 안식일에는 어떠한 일도 하지 못하게 하심
③ 죄를 용서하심

8. 유대인의 안식일에 대한 설명으로 알맞지 <u>않은</u> 것은?

① 안식일에 병자를 고치는 것은 허용되었다.
② 유대인들은 일요일을 안식일이라 불렀다.
③ 안식일에는 어떠한 일도 해서는 안된다.

9. 두 문장에 공통적으로 들어갈 말을 고르시오.

> Jesus looked with _____ at the poor litte dead girl.
> When Jesus saw the paralytic, he had _____ on him.

① pity   ② joy   ③ anxiety

Chapter Six

About six days after the miracle of the loaves and fish, Jesus climbed up a high mountain with only three of his closest disciples–Peter, James and John. While he was talking to them there, his appearance
5 was suddenly transformed into that of an angel.

His face shone like the noonday sun and the white of his garments sparkled like diamonds and silver.
10 Then, a bright cloud hovered over them and the disciples could hear a loud voice coming from the cloud. It said, "This is my
15 Son. I love him and am very pleased with him. Listen to him!" When they heard this, the disciples fell to the ground and

hid their faces because they were terrified. This miracle is called the Transfiguration of our Savior.

· ·

4 his appearance was suddenly transformed into that of an angel
그의 모습이 갑자기 천사로 변하였다.

6 His face shone like the noonday sun and the white of his garments sparkled like diamonds and silver.
그의 얼굴은 정오의 태양처럼 광채가 났고, 그의 하얀 의복은 다이아몬드와 은처럼 반짝거렸다.

예수님의 변화된 모습을
묘사하기 위해 비유적으로 쓰인
단어를 보기에서 모두 고르시오.

the noonday sun, garments,
that of an angel, cloud,
diamonds and silver, face

ANS. the noonday sun, that of an angel, diamonds and silver

Later, when they came back down the mountain, the disciples asked him, "Teacher, who is the greatest in the kingdom of heaven?"

Jesus then called a little child over to him and
5 answered, "A child like this is supreme in my Father's kingdom. And I assure you, that no one can see God unless they become humble and innocent like this little child. Whoever welcomes a child with love in my name welcomes me and my Father who
10 sent me. But anyone who harms a child will be punished so severely that it would be better if he had never been born. Children have guardian angels in heaven that are always watching over them." Our Savior loved all children and everyone in the world.
15 There has never been anyone who loved people as sincerely and completely as he did.

On a different occasion, Peter, the eldest disciple, asked Jesus, "If someone offends me, how many times should I forgive him? Seven times?"

20   He answered, "No, you must not put a limit on how many times you forgive. Be willing to forgive as often as someone apologizes to you. How can you

hope for mercy unless you show mercy?" Then he told his disciples a story about an unforgiving servant.

supreme 최고의, 가장 중요한	occasion 경우
assure 보증하다, 확실하게 하다	offend 기분을 상하게 하다,
whoever …하는 사람은 누구나	성나게 하다
severely 심하게	put a limit on 제한을 두다
guardian angel 수호천사	be willing to 기꺼이 …하다
completely 완벽하게, 온전히	unforgiving 용서하지 않는

· ·

6 I assure you, that no one can see God unless they become
humble and innocent like this little child
장담컨대, 이 어린아이처럼 겸손하고 순수하지 못하면 아무도 하나님을 보지
못할 것이다.

8 Whoever welcomes a child with love in my name
누구든지 사랑을 가지고 내 이름으로 어린아이를 영접하는 자는

10 anyone who harms a child will be punished so severely that it
would be better if he had never been born
어린아이를 해하는 자는 누구나 심한 벌을 받게 될 것이므로
차라리 태어나지 않았던 편이 나을 것이다.

21 Be willing to forgive as often as someone
apologizes to you.
사과를 받는 만큼이나 자주 기꺼이 (남을)
용서하도록 하여라.

According to Jesus, who is the
greatest in the kingdom of
heaven? Write in English.

45

"There once was a servant who owed his master a lot of money but he couldn't pay it back. His master was very angry and threatened to sell 5 him as a slave in some far away country. But the servant knelt down in agony and pleaded with his master to forgive him. The master finally relented and promised to forget about the debt. A little while later, the same servant met one 10 of his own servants who owed him a lot of money. Instead of being kind and generous to his servant like his master was to him, he had him thrown into jail until he paid back what he owed.

When his master heard about this, he was 15 furious and said, 'You worthless swine! I forgave you when you begged me to but you didn't do the same for your own servant!' So, he had the man taken to his prison where he was tortured until he paid back every penny." 20

Then Jesus said, "It is not right to expect God to forgive you if you don't forgive others." This is what that part of The Lord's Prayer means where it says "forgive us our sins as we forgive those who sin against us."

master 주인	relent[rilént] 가엾게 생각하다
pay back 갚다	furious 격한
threaten 위협하다	worthless 무가치한
slave 노예	swine 야비한 녀석, 탐욕자
in agony 번민하여, 고민하여	torture 괴롭히다, 고문하다
plead 간청하다	penny 1센트 동전, 푼돈

. . . .

7 the servant knelt down in agony
그 하인은 괴로워하며 무릎을 꿇었다.

12 Instead of being kind and generous to his servant like his master was to him,
그의 주인이 그에게 했던 것처럼 친절과 관용을 베푸는 대신에

14 until he paid back what he owed 그가 빚진 것을 갚을 때까지

18 he had the man taken to his prison where he was tortured until he paid back every penny 그가 푼돈 하나라도 다 갚을 때까지 그를 감옥에 집어넣어 고난받게 하였다.

22 This is what that part of The Lord's Prayer means where it says "forgive us our sins as we forgive those who sin against us."
이것이 주기도문에서 "우리에게 죄 지은 자를 용서한 것처럼 우리의 죄를 사하여 주옵시고"
라고 말하는 부분이 의미하는 바이다.

본문에 등장하는 악한 종의 결말은?

① 모든 빚을 다 갚을 때까지 감옥에 갇힘
② 평생을 노예로 살아가야 함
③ 지옥에 감

ANS. ①

Chapter Seven

As our Savior sat teaching the people and answering their questions, a lawyer stood up who wanted to test Jesus's knowledge of Jewish law. He asked, "Teacher, what do I have to do in order to go to heaven when I die?" 5

Jesus answered, "Keep the commandments of our faith that you have been taught from the time you were a child. The first and 10 most important commandment is that you must love God with all your heart, soul, mind and strength. The second is similar: you must love your neighbor as 15 yourself. There is no other commandment greater than these two."

Then the lawyer said, "But who is my neighbor? I really want to know."

Jesus answered him with a parable, which is a story that has a moral.

lawyer 변호사, 율법학자   parable 비유, 우화
commandment 율법, 계율   moral 교훈

. . . .

2 a lawyer stood up who wanted to test Jesus's knowledge of Jewish law 유대인의 법에 대한 그의 지식을 시험해보고 싶었던 한 율법학자가 서있었다.

4 what do I have to do in order to go to heaven when I die? 죽은 후에 천국에 가기 위해서는 우리가 무엇을 해야 합니까?

6 Keep the commandments of our faith that you have been taught from the time you were a child. 너희가 어렸을 때부터 배워왔던 믿음의 율법을 준수하여라.

15 you must love your neighbor as yourself
너 자신처럼 네 이웃을 사랑해야 한다.

According to Jesus, what is the most important?

① love   ② faith   ③ hope

"Once upon a time, there was a Jewish man traveling from Jerusalem to Jericho who was attacked by robbers. They stole his money and clothes, beat him up and left him half dead along 5 the side of the road.

After a while, a priest happened to pass by and saw the poor man lying there, but he paid no attention. Instead, he walked away quickly, more concerned about his own safety than about helping 10 the man. Later, a Levite, who assisted priests in a

temple, came walking by and he too saw the poor man lying by the road. He only looked at the man for a moment and then hurried away.

Jericho 여리고	concerned about …에 대해
priest 목사, 제사장	걱정하는
pass by 옆을 지나가다	Levite 레위 사람

. . . .

4 beat him up and left him half dead along the side of the road
때려서 반쯤 죽다시피 된 그를 길가에 내버려두고 갔다.

6 a priest happened to pass by and saw the poor man lying there,
어떤 제사장이 우연히 옆을 지나가다 그 불쌍한 사람이 거기에 누워있는
것을 보았다.

8 more concerned about his own safety
than about helping the man 그를 돕는
것보다는 자신의 안전을 더 염려하여

강도 당한 유대인을 보고 제사장과
레위인이 보인 공통적인 반응은?

① 모른 척하고 그냥 지나감
② 그를 데려다 치료해줌
③ 그를 위해 기도함

"Towards the evening, a foreigner from Samaria came riding down the road and saw the poor man. Now Samaritans and Jews have great animosity for one another because of their different religious
5 views. He felt he had to do something for him or he might die. So he bandaged his wounds, put him on his horse and took him to the nearest inn. The next morning, he gave the manager a large sum of money and said, 'I must go and tend to some business, but
10 please take care of this man until I get back. Any money you spend over this amount I've given you, will be repaid to you on my return."

Jesus turned to the lawyer and asked him, "Now who do you think was a true neighbor to the man who was mugged?"

"I suppose it was the man who took care of him."

"Right," replied our Savior. "Go and do the same. Be kind to everyone because all people are your neighbors."

Samaria 사마리아	wound 상처
Samaritan 사마리아 사람	a large sum of 많은 양의
animosity[ǽnimάsiti] 적대감	tend to 돌보다
bandage 붕대로 감다	mug (강도가) 습격하다

· ·

3 Samaritans and Jews have great animosity for one another
사마리아 사람들과 유대인들은 서로에게 굉장한 적대감을 가지고 있다.

5 He felt he had to do something for him or he might die.
그는 그를 위해 무언가를 하지 않는다면 그가 죽을지 모른다고 생각했다.

10 Any money you spend over this amount I've given you 제가 당신에게 준 것 외에 추가로 쓰여진 돈은 전부

2 who do you think was a true neighbor to the man who was mugged? 너는 강도 당한 사람의 진정한 이웃이 누구라고 생각하느냐?

예수님은 강도를 당한 유대인의 진정한 이웃은 누구라고 말씀하셨나?

① 레위인
② 바리새인
③ 사마리아인

One day, as our Savior was walking through the
city of Jericho, he saw a man up in a tree, who was
trying to get a better view. This man was very short
and he had to climb the tree to be able to see
5 through the crowd surrounding Jesus. His name was
Zacchaeus, and everyone in the city considered him
a common sinner. Jesus called out to him as he
passed by and said he would like to eat supper at
his house that evening. There were some Pharisees
10 and other disdainful men in the crowd who said
among themselves, "He eats with sinners!" Jesus
knew what they were saying and stopped to tell the
parable of the Prodigal Son.

"Long ago, there was a man who had two sons. The younger son came to his father one day and said, 'Give me my share of the inheritance now and let me go off and do whatever I please.' The father agreed and the son took his money and traveled to a far away country.

Jericho 여리고
view 시야, 전망
Zacchaeus 삭개오
disdainful 오만한, 경멸적인

prodigal[prɑ́dig(ə)l] 방탕한
share 몫
inheritance 유산
whatever 무엇이든

6 everyone in the city considered him a common sinner
그 도시에 있는 모든 사람들이 그를 비천한 죄인으로 생각했다.

7 Jesus called out to him as he passed by
예수께서는 옆으로 지나가시다가 그를 불러내셨다.

12 (Jesus) stopped to tell the parable of the Prodigal Son.
탕자에 대한 비유를 말씀하시려고 멈춰 서셨다.

3 Give me my share of the inheritance now and let me go off and do whatever I please. 이제 유산의 몫을 저에게 주셔서, 떠나서 내가 하고 싶은 것은 무엇이나 할 수 있게 해 주세요.'

삭개오에 대한 설명으로 옳지 않은 것은?

① 키가 작았다.
② 예수님을 만나기를 원했다.
③ 예수님의 제자였다.

ANS.3

"At first, the son enjoyed his indulgent lifestyle, but he quickly spent all his money on food, drink, women and gambling. Soon afterwards, there was a terrible economic crisis all throughout that country.
5 The earth dried up and nothing could grow, so famine spread across the land. The Prodigal Son was so desperate to survive that he took a job as a servant feeding pigs. In his extreme hunger, he thought even the pigs' food looked delicious, but his
10 master never offered to give him any. Finally, he reached the end of his rope and said to himself, 'Even my father's servants get decent meals while I'm here starving to death! I'm going to go back to my father and ask him to forgive me. Maybe he will
15 hire me as one of his servants!'

So, he made the long and difficult journey back again to his hometown. As he was coming down the road toward his father's house, his father caught sight of him. Though he looked terrible in his
20 miserable condition, his father recognized him and ran to greet him. He cried and hugged and kissed him. Then he ordered his servants to take care of

his son. They cleaned him up and dressed him in the most expensive clothes. The father ordered his cooks to prepare a grand banquet so that they could revel in his son's return.

indulgent 방탕한	hire 고용하다
gambling 도박	catch sight of ···를 찾아내다
economic 경제적인	miserable 비참한
famine[fǽmin] 기근	greet 인사하다
desperate 필사적인, 절박한	banquet 연회, 향연, 축제
decent 웬만한, 남부끄럽지 않은	revel[révl] 한껏 즐기다,
be starving to death 굶어 죽다	매우 기뻐하다

. . . .

2 he quickly spent all his money on food, drink, women and gambling 그는 곧 모든 돈을 먹는 것과, 술과 여자와 도박에 탕진해 버렸다.

6 The Prodigal Son was so desperate to survive that he took a job as a servant feeding pigs. 그 탕자는 살아남기 위해 너무 절박한 나머지 돼지를 먹이는 하인으로 일을 하게 되었다.

10 Finally, he reached the end of his rope 마침내 그는 벼랑 끝에 놓이게 되었다.

12 Even my father's servants get decent meals while I'm here starving to death! 심지어 내 아버지의 하인들도 웬만한 식사는 하는데 나는 여기서 굶어 죽게 되었구나!

3 so that they could revel in his son's return 그 아들의 귀향을 기뻐할 수 있도록

탕자가 돼지치기 하인으로 일했던 이유는?

① 돈을 도둑 맞았기 때문에
② 돈을 다 탕진했기 때문에
③ 아버지가 시켜서

"Later that evening, the older son came back to the house after working hard all day. He heard music and saw people dancing, so he asked one of the servants what was going on. The servant told him everything that had happened to his younger brother, which is why his father wanted everyone to celebrate. Hearing this, the older brother was indignant and wouldn't go into the house. When his father saw him standing outside, he tried to persuade him to come in and join the party.

'Father,' he said, 'you aren't fair! All these years I've stayed here and worked for you, but you never honored me. Then, my younger brother returns after spending all his money on dissolute living, and you are so excited, you want to celebrate!'

'Son,' said the father, 'I know you have always been with me, and all that I have is yours. But I thought your brother must have died when I heard about what happened in that country he was living in. Today I found that he is alive. He was lost and has been found. It's only right that we should give thanks and rejoice because of his safe return home."

This story was meant to teach that no matter what you've done, God will always forgive you and welcome you back. All that is required is for you to be sorry for your sins.

indignant 분개한
persuade 설득하다
honor 존중하다, …에게 경의를
  표하다

dissolute [dísəlùːt] 방탕한,
  방종한
rejoice at …에 기뻐하다

· ·

6 which is why his father wanted everyone to celebrate
  그것이 그의 아버지가 모든 이들이 축하해 주기를 바라는 연유이다.

7 Hearing this, the older brother was indignant
  이 말을 듣고 그의 형은 분개하였다.

11 All these years I've stayed here and worked for you,
  이 모든 세월동안 저는 여기에 머물러 아버지를 위해 일했습니다.

18 your brother must have died 너의 동생은 죽었음에 틀림없다.

1 This story was meant to teach that no matter what you've
  done, God will always forgive you and welcome you back.
  이것은 너희가 무엇을 하든지 간에 하나님은 항상 너희를 용서
  하시고 너희의 돌아옴을 기뻐하신다는
  것을 가르치기 위한 이야기였다.

3 All that is required is for you to be
  sorry for your sins. 필요한 것은 너희
  죄에 대한 회개일 뿐이다.

윗 글의 내용과 일치하면 T,
일치하지 않으면 F로 표시하시오.

– The older son also rejoiced
  at his brother's safe return
  home. (   )

– The father forgave the
  Prodigal Son. (   )

59

ANS. F, T

The Pharisees who came to hear Jesus preach, listened to his parables with closed minds. They were rich, greedy and arrogant. As a warning to them, he told the parable of Lazarus and the rich
5 man. "There was once a rich man who always wore the most exquisite clothing and dined extravagantly every day. There was also a beggar, named Lazarus, who had a horrid skin disease. He lay down by the rich man's front gate hoping to receive some of the
10 leftovers from his meals. Eventually the beggar died and was carried to heaven by the angels. In heaven Abraham, a very holy man who lived a long time before Lazarus, welcomed him. Then the rich man died, was buried and went to hell. From his place of
15 torment, he looked up and saw Abraham far away in heaven, and Lazarus was with him. He cried out,

'Abraham, have mercy on me! Send Lazarus down here to give me something to drink. It's so hot here and the flames
20 are killing me!'

But Abraham said, 'Remember that in your life on earth you enjoyed many luxuries but Lazarus was a poor beggar. Now he is being comforted and you are suffering!"

greedy 탐욕스러운
arrogant 오만한, 거만한
Lazarus 나사로
exquisite [ékskwizit] 훌륭한, 우아한
extravagantly 낭비적으로
horrid 매우 불쾌한, 무서운
Abraham 아브라함
torment 고통, 고문
flame 불길, 불꽃, 화염

· ·

9 hoping to receive some of the leftovers from his meals
그의 식사에서 남은 음식의 일부라도 얻기를 바라며

11 In heaven Abraham, a very holy man who lived a long time before Lazarus, welcomed him. 나사로보다 오래 전에 살았던 거룩한 사람인 아브라함이 천국에서 그를 반갑게 맞이하였다.

14 From his place of torment, he looked up
고통의 상황 속에서 그는 위를 올려다보았다.

1 Now he is being comforted and you are suffering! 그는 이제 위로를 받고 있고 당신은 고통을 당하고 있다!

밑줄친 부분과
바꾸어 쓸 수 <u>없는</u> 표현은?

Now he is being comforted
and you are suffering!

① happy - miserable
② blessed - cursed
③ working - resting

ANS. ③

Jesus also told the Pharisees about two men who went to a temple to pray. One was a Pharisee and the other was a government tax collector. 5 Tax collectors were despised by the Jews because they worked for the oppressive Roman government. The Pharisee looked up to heaven and said, "God, I thank you 10 that I am better than other men, and especially, that I'm not like this tax collector!"

The tax collector stood in the back of the temple and didn't dare to raise his eyes up to heaven. Instead, he beat his breast and said, "God, have 15 mercy on me, a sinner!"

Jesus told them that God was merciful to the tax collector and was pleased with his prayer because he prayed with a humble and sincere heart.

tax collector 세무원(세리) Roman 로마의
despise [dispáiz] 경멸하다 dare to 감히 …하다
oppressive 압제적인, 압박하는

. . . .

3 One was a Pharisee and the other was a government tax
collector. 한 사람은 바리새인이었고, 또 다른 사람은 정부의 세리(세무원)
였다.

12 I'm not like this tax collector!
저는 이 세리와 같은 사람이 아닙니다!

14 (The tax collector) didn't dare to raise his eyes up to heaven
그 세리는 감히 눈을 들어 하늘을 올려다보지 못했다.

빈칸에 알맞은
말을 고르시오.

Why God was pleased
with tax collector's prayer is
that he was _____ while
the Pharisee was _____.

① humble - proud
② sad - happy
③ polite - rude

ANS. ①

The Pharisees were outraged when they heard Jesus talk like that, so they began plotting against him. They sent some spies to ask him questions that would force him to say something that was 5 against the Roman or Jewish law. On one occasion, the spies tried to get Jesus to speak out against the Roman Emperor Caesar, who ruled almost the whole world at that time. Caesar demanded everyone pay a special tribute tax to him, and anyone who 10 refused would face serious consequences. The spies wanted to force Jesus to say that the tax was not right, which would cause him to be thrown in prison or possibly executed.

They came up to him and said, "Teacher, you are 15 an expert about God's law and you don't respect people just because they are rich or powerful. Tell us, is it right that we have to pay the tribute tax to Caesar?"

Now, Jesus knew what they were thinking and 20 so he answered, "Why do you ask me such a simple question? Show me a coin." Someone in the crowd handed him a coin. "Whose picture and whose name is on this coin?" he asked them.

They all said, "Caesar's."

"Then," he said, "give to Caesar what belongs to him."

outrage 격분시키다, 충격을 주다	demand 요구하다
plot against …를 해하려고 음모를 꾸미다	tribute[tríbjuːt] 공물, 조세
	consequence 결과
force 강요하다, 억지로 시키다	execute[éksikjùːt] 사형시키다
Caesar 시저	expert 전문가

. . . .

3 questions that would force him to say something that was against the Roman or Jewish law
어쩔 수 없이 로마나 유대인 법을 어기는 것을 말하게 하는 질문

6 get Jesus to speak out against the Roman Emperor Caesar,
예수께 로마 황제 시저를 거스르는 말을 공공연하게 하게 하다.

10 The spies wanted to force Jesus to say that the tax was not right, which would cause him to be thrown in prison or possibly executed. 그 스파이들은 예수께 세금 내는 것은 옳지 않다라고 어쩔 수 없이 말하게 하려 했는데, 그렇게 말한다면 그는 감옥에 갇히거나 사형을 당하게 될지도 모른다.

3 give to Caesar what belongs to him
시저에게 속한 것은 그에게 바치시오.

세금 문제를 예수께 질문한 까닭은?

① 세금에 대한 자문을 구하고자
② 예수님을 곤경에 빠뜨리고자
③ 세금 내는 것을 원치 않았기 때문에

The spies were frustrated and disappointed that they couldn't trap Jesus and they went away. Our Savior knew
5 their hearts and thoughts, and he knew that other men were planning to trip him up so they could find a way to have him put to death.

10   On that day, as he was teaching them, Jesus sat near the Public Treasury. There were many wealthy people passing by, putting large amounts of money in a collection box with much pomp and circumstance. There was also a poor widow who
15 came by and dropped two pennies into the box, then went quietly away. Jesus saw this and pointed out to his disciples that the poor widow had given more than anyone else. The other people were rich and would never miss the money they contributed,
20 but the widow gave all she had. He told them not to forget what the widow did when they thought they were doing something charitable.

frustrated 실망한, 좌절된
disappointed 실망한
trap 함정에 빠뜨리다,
　　　곤궁한 처지에 몰다
trip up 걸려서 넘어지게 하다
treasury 자금, 기금
with much pomp and
circumstance 당당하게 격식을
　　　　　　　갖추고
widow 과부
contribute 기부하다
charitable 자선의, 박애의

. . . .

4 knew their hearts and thoughts
그들의 심정과 생각을 아셨다.

8 so they could find a way to have him put to death
그를 사형시킬 방법을 찾기 위해

11 There were many wealthy people passing by, putting large
amounts of money in a collection box with much pomp and
circumstance.
당당하게 모금함에 많은 돈을 넣고 지나가는 부유한 사람들이 많았다.

19 (The other people) would never miss the money they
contributed,
다른 사람들은 그들이 기부한 그 돈이 결코 아쉽지
않을 것이다.

According to Jesus, who
gave the most to God?

① many wealthy people
② his disciples
③ a poor widow

Chapter Eight

There was a man named Lazarus from Bethany, which is a town near Jerusalem, who was on the verge of death. He was the brother of Mary Magdalene, the woman who had cleaned Jesus's feet 5 with her tears and dried them with her hair. She and her sister Martha sent a message to Jesus saying that their brother was sick and could die at any time. He did not respond to their message until two days later. Then he said to his disciples, "Let's go to 10 Bethany. Lazarus is dead." When they arrived there, they found out Lazarus had died four days earlier and had already been buried.

Martha heard that Jesus was on his way to their house, so she got up and ran to meet him, leaving 15 her sister Mary with all the neighbors who had come to comfort them. As soon as she saw him, she burst into tears and said, "Lord, if only you had been here, my brother wouldn't have died!"

"Your brother will come to life again," replied our Savior.

"I know he will on the Day of Resurrection at the end of the world," said Martha.

Jesus told her, "I am the Resurrection and the Life. Do you believe me?"

"Yes, Lord," she answered, and then she ran back to tell Mary that Jesus was coming.

Lazarus 나사로
Bethany 베다니
Martha 마르다
at any time 금방이라도

respond 반응하다
bury[béri] 묻다, 매장하다
resurrection[rèzərékʃ(ə)n]
　　　　부활, 소생

· ·

2 who was on the verge of death 죽음이 임박했던
8 He did not respond to their message until two days later.
　그는 이틀이 지나고서야 비로소 그 전갈에 응답을 하셨다.
17 if only you had been here, my brother wouldn't
　have died! 당신이 여기 계시기만 했더라도 오라비
　는 죽지 않았을 것입니다!
4 he will on the Day of Resurrection at
　the end of the world, 세상 끝
　부활의 날에 그가 살아날
　것입니다.

다음 말씀의 의미는 무엇인가?

"I am the Resurrection and the Life. Do you believe me?"

① 부활의 날 Lazarus는 살아날 것이다.
② 내가 Lazarus를 살릴 수 있다. 걱정
　말아라.
③ 죽고 사는 것은 하늘에 달렸다.

ANS. ②

When Mary heard this, she hurried out of the house, followed by everyone who was visiting. Coming up to him, she fell down at his feet and began crying, as did all the rest of the people. Jesus
5 was so moved that he cried, too. Then he asked,

"Where have you buried him?"

They said, "Lord, come and see!"

He was placed in a cave not too far away, and there was a big stone covering the entrance. When
10 they all reached the tomb, Jesus told some of the men to roll the stone away. He then looked up to heaven, gave thanks to God and shouted, "Lazarus, come out!" The dead man came back to life and walked out of the cave. Seeing what had happened,
15 many of the people there believed that Jesus

was truly the Son of God who came to save all mankind. Others who witnessed this miracle ran off to tell the Pharisees. From that day on, they resolved to prevent more people from believing in him and started making plans how to kill him. They agreed among themselves that if Jesus came to Jerusalem before the Feast of Passover, which was to be held soon, he must be arrested.

---

roll away 굴리다
come back to life 살아나다
mankind 인류
from that day on 그날부터

resolve[rizólv] 결심하다
the Feast of Passover 유월절
　　　　　　　　　　　　축제(향연)
arrest 체포하다

· ·

2 followed by everyone who was visiting 방문객 모두가 그녀의 뒤를 따랐다.

4 as did all the rest of the people 나머지 사람들 모두가 그랬던 것처럼

14 Seeing what had happened, 일어난 일을 목격하고서

3 they resolved to prevent more people from believing in him 그들은 더 많은 사람들이 그를 믿는 것을 막아야겠다고 결심했다.

7 the Feast of Passover, which was to be held soon, 곧 열리게 될 유월절 축제

밑줄 친 부분과 바꿔 쓸 수 있는 말이 <u>아닌</u> 것은?

They resolved to <u>prevent</u> more people from believing in him.

① stop ② keep ③ push

ANS:③

The Feast of Passover was just around the corner, and Jesus, along with his disciples, traveled towards Jerusalem. While they were still outside the city, he pointed to a little village nearby and told two of his disciples to go there and get things ready for his triumphal entry. He said they would find a young donkey tied to a tree, which they were to bring to him. If anyone asked questions about what they were doing, they were supposed to say, "The Lord needs it." Inside the village, they found everything just as Jesus had said, and so they brought the donkey to him. He mounted the animal and rode it into Jerusalem. All around him was a huge crowd of people throwing down their robes on the ground

and waving palm branches. They made a path for him to get through and shouted as he rode by, "Hosanna to the Son of David! (David was

a great king in Jerusalem a long time ago.) Give
praise to him who comes in the name of God!"

just around the corner   robe 길고 품이 큰 겉옷, 의복
                 가까운, 임박한   palm branch 종려나무 가지
triumphal entry 개선 입성식   Hosanna 호산나(신을 찬미하는 말)

. . . .

4 told two of his disciples to go there and get things ready for his
  triumphal entry 제자 중 두 명에게 거기에 가서 개선 입성식을 위해
  준비를 하라고 명하셨다.

6 a young donkey tied to a tree, which they were to bring to him
  그에게 가져가기로 되어 있었던 나무에 묶여 있던 어린 당나귀

13 All around him was a huge crowd of people throwing down
   their robes on the ground and waving palm branches.
   의복을 던져 바닥에 깔고 종려나무 가지를 흔드는 수많은
   사람들의 무리가 그 주위를 에워싸고 있었다.

예루살렘으로 입성하신 예수님을 맞는
군중들의 반응으로 옳지 <u>않은</u> 것은?

① 종려나무 가지를 흔들며 환영함
② 호산나, 다윗의 아들이라고 외침
③ 그를 죽이려고 폭력을 휘두름

Jesus made his way to the temple, and when he got there, he was furious with what he saw. All at once, he started throwing over the tables where the money-exchangers sat and knocked over the cages
5 of animals being sold there for sin offerings. He even took a whip and started beating the salesmen and tax collectors! As he went along, he shouted,

"My Father's house is sacred but you have made it into a market place!"

10 Everyone who had followed Jesus to the temple cried out, "This is Jesus, the prophet of Nazareth!" Many blind and lame people came running over to him to be healed. The priests and Pharisees wanted to arrest him, but were afraid of how the crowd
15 might react. Meanwhile, Jesus kept healing the sick and teaching the people out in the open. At night, he stayed in Bethany since it was in the vicinity of Jerusalem.

make one's way to
　　　　…로 나아가다

all at once 갑자기
money-exchanger 환전수
knock over 뒤집어엎다
sin offering 속죄 제물
　　(죄를 용서받기 위해 드리는 제물)

whip 채찍
sacred 신성한, 거룩한
prophet [práfit] 예언자
lame 절름발이의, 불구의
react 반응하다
meanwhile 그 동안, 그 사이에
in the vicinity of …의 부근에(의)

• •

2 he was furious with what he saw 그는 그가 본 광경에 격분하였다.

3 started throwing over the tables 탁자를 내던지기 시작했다.

4 knocked over the cages of animals being sold there for sin
offerings 속죄 제물로 거기서 팔리고 있는 동물들의 우리를 쳐서
넘어 뜨렸다.

12 came running over to him to be healed
치료를 받기 위해 그에게로 달려 왔다.

14 (The priests and Pharisees) were afraid of how the crowd might
react 군중들이 어떻게 반응할지가 두려웠다.

15 Jesus kept healing the sick and teaching the people out in the
open 예수께서는 계속해서 병든 자를 고치시고 공공장소에서 사람들을
가르치셨다.

17 since it was in the vicinity of Jerusalem
그곳이 예루살렘에서 가까웠기 때문에

예루살렘으로 입성했던 날 밤
예수님이 묵은 곳은?

① Bethany
② Jerusalem
③ Nazareth

75

ANS. ①

The feast of Passover arrived and Jesus said to two of his disciples, "Go into Jerusalem and you will meet a man carrying a pitcher of water. Follow him to his house and say to him, 'The Lord wants to
5 know if the room is ready where he will eat the passover meal with his disciples.' He will show you a large fully-furnished room on the second floor of his house. Then go and prepare the things we will need for the supper."

10 When the two disciples went into the city, everything was just as Jesus had said it would be. They met the man with the water and went to his house, where he showed them the upper room.

After they had finished preparing for the supper, Jesus and his other disciples came and they all sat down together to share the Passover meal. It is always called The Last Supper, because this was the last time that Jesus ate and drank with his disciples.

pitcher 물주전자
fully-furnished 완전히 가구를
           갖춘
upper 윗층의

share 나누다
the Last Supper 최후의 만찬
           (예수님과 그의 제자들이 함께
           나눈 마지막 식사)

. . . .

5 if the room is ready where he will eat the passover
  meal with his disciples 예수님께서 제자들과 함께
  유월적 식사를 하실 방이 준비가 되었는지
11 everything was just as Jesus had said
  it would be 모든 것이 예수께서
  말씀하신 그대로였다.

최후의 만찬이 이루어진 장소에 대한
설명으로 알맞지 않은 것은?

① 이층방이다.
② 보통 때 예배를 드리는 곳이다.
③ 크고 많은 가구가 있는 방이다.

ANS.2

During the meal, Jesus got up, took a cloth and a large bowl of water, and began washing his disciples' feet. Peter, the oldest disciple, didn't want Jesus to wash his feet. Our Savior told him that he 5 was doing this to give them an example of what it means to serve. He wanted them to always remember to respect one another and never to be proud or quarrelsome.

Then, he became sad as he looked around at his 10 disciples and said, "There is someone here who is going to betray me."

They were all shocked and asked Jesus, "Who is it? Is it me, Lord?"

He answered, "It is the one who dips his bread 15 into the sauce dish at the same time as I do."

Again, Jesus answered, "It is the man who I will give a piece of bread to after dipping it in the sauce dish."

Right after he finished speaking, he took a piece 20 of bread, dipped it into the dish and handed it to Judas Iscariot saying, "Do what you have to do quickly." The other disciples didn't understand, but

Judas realized that Jesus knew what he was planning to do. So, he went out into the night to meet with some priests and Pharisees. He said to them, "What will you give me if I hand Jesus over to you?" They offered to pay him thirty pieces of silver. For this sum of money, Judas agreed to betray our Savior.

serve (신, 사람 등을) 섬기다   dip 담그다
quarrelsome 싸우기를 좋아하는,   Judas 유다(예수의 제자 중 한 사람)
                시비조의   hand over 넘겨주다
betray[bitréi] 배신하다

. . . .

5 to give them an example of what it means to serve
   섬긴다는 것이 무엇을 뜻하는지 그들에게 본보기를 보여주시기
   위해
15 at the same time as I do 나와 동시에
16 It is the man who I will give a piece of
   bread to 내가 빵 조각을 건네는 사람이
   바로 그 사람이다.
21 Do what you have to do
   quickly. 네가 해야만
   하는 일을 신속히
   행하여라.

예수께서 제자들의 발을 씻기신 이유는?

① 섬김의 본을 보이시려고
② 청결을 강조하시고자
③ 본래 스승이 식사 전에 해 주는
   일이므로

Comprehension

Checkup II

1. According to Jesus, what is the most important commandment? Write in English.

2. 예수께서 삭개오의 집에 머물겠다고 말씀하신 이유는?

① 예수님을 만나고자 하는 삭개오의 노력을 귀하게 여기셨기 때문에

② 삭개오가 부자였기 때문에

③ 삭개오를 자신의 제자로 만드시기 위해

3. 다음은 누구에 대한 설명인가?

> They were considered proud and arrogant by Jesus. They made plans to kill Jesus. They thought nobody was supposed to do any kind of work at all on the Sabbath.

① Pharisees   ② disciples   ③ prophets

4. According to Jesus, how many times should we forgive others?

① never

② limitless

③ just when someone apologizes to us

5. 다음은 탕자의 비유가 주는 교훈이다. 빈 칸에 들어갈 알맞은 말로 짝지어진 것은?

> No matter what you have done, God will always
> _____ you and _____ you back.

① punish - return
② forgive - welcome
③ scold - push

6. 빚을 탕감받은 종의 비유에 적절한 속담은?

① Treat others as you want to be treated.
② Easier said than done.
③ The early bird catches the worm.

7. Who is a true neighbor in the parable of a Jewish man attacked by robbers?

① a priest
② a Levite
③ a Samaritan

8. Jesus loves children because they _____.

① are humble and innocent
② love him so dearly
③ have strong faith in him

정답은 p.128에

Chapter Nine

Later, during the course of the meal, our Savior took a loaf of bread from the table, blessed it, broke it into pieces and gave some to each of the disciples. Then, he took a cup of wine, blessed it and gave it
5 to them saying, "Do this in memory of me!" After they had finished supper and had sung a song, they went out into the Garden of Gesthemane, located on the Mount of Olives just outside the city. When they got there, Jesus told his disciples that he would

be arrested that night and that they would all abandon him. But Peter protested that he would never leave his side.

"Before the rooster crows in the morning," Jesus replied, "you will disown me three times."

Peter insisted, "Never, Lord! Even if I have to die with you, I will never deny you!" All the other disciples said the same thing.

in memory of …의 기념으로	rooster 수탉
Garden of Gesthemane 겟세마네 정원	crow 울다
Mount of Olives 올리브 동산	disown[disóun] 부인하다, 관계가 없다고 말하다
abandon 버리다	insist 주장하다
protest 항의하다, 항변하다	deny 부인하다

. . . .

5 Do this in memory of me! 나를 기념하여 이것을 행하여라.
2 he would never leave his side 결코 그의 곁을 떠나지 않겠다고
6 Even if I have to die with you, 제가 당신과 함께 죽어야만 한다고 해도

예수께서 Peter에 대해 예언하신 일은 무엇인가?

① 예수를 세 번 부인할 것이다.
② 끝까지 예수를 따를 것이다.
③ 예수와 함께 감옥에 갇힐 것이다.

ANS. ①

Jesus then led them over to a quiet part of the garden and told them to keep watch. He left them and went off by himself to pray. As the disciples were exhausted, they soon fell asleep but Jesus 5 remained awake praying intensely. He knew about the wicked men who were going to kill him and he cried out loud to God in pain. His grief and mental distress was so severe that he sweat drops of blood. After finishing his prayers he went back to the 10 disciples and said, "Get up! We must leave this place! The man who is going to betray me is near!"

Now, Judas was familiar with that garden because our Savior often took long walks there with his disciples. He knew just where to find Jesus. 15 With him was a group of soldiers and military

officers who had been dispatched by the priests and Pharisees. It was dark, so they carried lanterns to help them find their way. They carried swords and chains too because they didn't know if there would be an angry mob who would try to protect Jesus.

exhausted 매우 지친, 피곤한
intensely 격렬하게, 맹렬히
wicked 사악한
grief 슬픔
mental 정신적인
distress 고통, 고민, 걱정

severe 심한
be familiar with …와 친숙하다,
                  …을 잘 알다
dispatch[dispǽtʃ] 급송하다,
                  급파하다
mob 군중, 폭도

• •

2 told them to keep watch 그들에게 망을 보라고 말씀하셨다.
2 He left them and went off by himself to pray.
   그는 그들을 남겨둔 채, 홀로 기도하러 가셨다.
4 Jesus remained awake praying intensely
   예수께서는 간절히 기도하시며 깨어 계셨다.
7 His grief and mental distress was so severe that he
   sweat drops of blood. 그의 슬픔과 정신적 고통이
   너무나 격심하여 피땀을 흘렸다.
14 He knew just where to find Jesus.
   그는 예수를 어디서 찾을 수 있을지
   바로 알았다.

예수님을 제사장들과 바리새인들에
게 팔아 넘긴 제자는 누구인가?

① Peter   ② Judas   ③ John

Just as Jesus and the disciples were about to leave the garden, Judas and the soldiers caught sight of them. Because they didn't know what Jesus looked like, Judas said, "The man I walk up to and greet with a kiss is the one you are to arrest."

Jesus then asked, "Who are you looking for?"

"Jesus of Nazareth," they answered.

"I am he. Let my disciples go freely. I am the one you want."

Then, Judas stepped forward and kissed him saying, "Hello, Master!"

Jesus responded by asking, "Judas, are you betraying me with a kiss?"

Suddenly, the soldiers rushed over and seized him. No one attempted to put up a struggle to protect him except Peter, who cut off the right ear of one of the high priests' servants with his pocket knife. But Jesus told him to

put the knife away, and then he healed the servant's ear. After that, he surrendered himself to the soldiers. At this, all of the disciples deserted him and ran off into the darkness. Not one of them
5 stayed by his side.

be about to 막 …하려고 하다
catch sight of 찾다, 발견하다
attempt 시도하다
put up a struggle 투쟁을 벌이다
put away 치우다
surrender oneself to …에게
자신을 내어주다, 넘겨주다
desert[dizə́:rt] 버리다

··

1 Just as Jesus and the disciples were about to leave the garden,
예수님과 제자들이 막 정원을 떠나려 했을 때

5 the one you are to arrest 당신들이 체포해야 하는 바로 그 사람

15 No one attempted to put up a struggle to protect him except Peter, 베드로를 제외하고는 아무도 싸워서 그 분을 보호하려고 하지 않았다.

3 At this, all of the disciples deserted him and ran off into the darkness.
이것을 보고 모든 제자들이 그를 버렸고 어둠 속으로 도망쳤다.

윗글의 내용과 일치하지 않는 것은?

① 예수께서는 자신이 체포당할 것을 이미 알고 계셨다.
② Peter를 제외하고는 아무도 예수님을 보호하려고 하지 않았다.
③ 군인들은 제자들이 두려워 예수님을 체포하지 못했다.

ANS. 3

Chapter Ten

After a while, Peter and another disciple felt such remorse about what had happened that they decided to follow our Savior at a distance to see what would happen. They reached the house of the
5 High Priest, Caiaphas, and Jesus was taken inside. Assembled there were many important Jewish leaders, priests and Pharisees who wanted to interrogate him. Peter stood outside by the front gate, too, afraid at first to go in. Then, he asked one
10 of the servant girls to let him and his friend into the yard so they could hear what was going on. The servant looked at him suspiciously and asked,

"Aren't you one of the disciples?"

He answered, "No, I'm not!" So, she let them in
15 and they went over to the bonfire to warm themselves.

remorse 후회, 양심의 가책
at a distance 멀리서
Caiaphas 가야바(대제사장)
assemble 모이다, 회합하다

interrogate [intérəgeit]
　　　심문하다, 문초하다
suspiciously 의심스럽게
bonfire 모닥불

. . . .

1 felt such remorse about what had happened that they decided
to follow our Savior at a distance 일어났던 일에 대해 너무나 큰 양심
의 가책을 느껴서 그들은 멀리서 우리의 구세주를 따라 가리라 마음먹었다.

6 Assembled there were many important Jewish leaders, priests
and Pharisees 많은 중요한 유대인 지도자들, 제사장들, 그리고
바리새인들이 거기에 모여 있었다.

11 so they could hear what was going on
무슨 일이 진행되고 있는지를 들을 수 있도록

　　　　　　　Caiaphas의 집에 있었던 사람이
아닌 것은?

① 유대인 지도자들
② 예수님의 어머님
③ 바리새인들

89

There were servants and soldiers crowded around the fire because it was bitter cold that night. Some of these men asked Peter the same question as the servant girl saying, "You must be one of his
5 disciples! Your northern accent gives you away."

He protested angrily and shouted, "No, I'm not!"

One of those men, who was related to the servant whose ear Peter had cut off, said, "Didn't I see you in the garden with him?"

10 Peter professed, "I swear, I don't know the man!" Immediately a rooster crowed in the distance and Peter recalled what Jesus had said to him earlier that night. He stumbled outside, unable to see clearly because of the hot tears streaming down his face,
15 and fell to his knees in anguish.

bitter cold 몹시 추운
give away 들춰내다, 폭로하다
be related to …과 관련이 있다
profess[prəfés] 공언하다, 주장하다
swear 맹세하다
in the distance 멀리서

recall 회상하다
stumble 비틀거리다
clearly 명확하게, 선명하게
stream down 흘러내리다
fall to one's knees 무릎을 꿇다
in anguish 괴로워서, 괴로운 나머지

• •

3 the same question as the servant girl
하녀가 물었던 것과 동일한 질문
5 Your northern accent gives you away.
당신의 북부 억양을 들으면 다 알 수 있어요.
7 One of those men, who was related to the servant whose ear
Peter had cut off,
베드로가 귀를 잘라버렸던 하인과 관련된 사람 중 한 명이
13 He stumbled outside, unable to see clearly
그는 똑똑히 볼 수가 없어서 비틀거리며 밖으로 나왔다.

Peter를 알아보는 하녀에게 보인
Peter의 반응이 아닌 것은?

① 화를 냄
② 예수님을 모른다고 부인함
③ 눈물을 흘리면서 시인함

The High Priest and other Jewish leaders queried Jesus at length about his teachings. He answered that he had always taught in public places for everyone to hear. So if they really wanted to know 5 what he said, they should ask the people who heard him. One of the soldiers thought it was rude for Jesus to talk that way to the High Priest and slapped his face with the back of his hand. Then, two men were brought in who were paid to tell lies about 10 Jesus. They said they heard him say that he could tear down the temple and rebuild it in three days. Jesus refused to comment on the accusation, but the priests and Pharisees all agreed that he was guilty of blasphemy and should be sentenced to death.

15 When Judas Iscariot realized that our Savior was going to be put to death, he was so guilt-ridden for having him arrested that he gave back the thirty pieces of silver to the priests. He said, "I have betrayed an innocent man!" Then he ran out of the 20 house and, in despair, committed suicide. The priests didn't know what to do with the money, so they bought the plot of land where Judas hanged

himself and turned it into a cemetery for foreigners. They called it "The Potter's Field" but in the future, it came to be known as "The Field of Blood."

query 묻다, 의심하다	be put to death 사형에 처해지다
slap 찰싹 때리다	guilt-ridden 죄의식에 시달린,
tear down (건물을) 헐다	죄의식에 고통받는
comment 비평하다, 주석을 달다	in despair 자포자기하여
accusation 고발, 고소	commit 범하다, 저지르다
guilty 죄를 범한, 유죄의	suicide 자살
blasphemy [blǽsfimi]	plot 작은 터
불경, 신성모독	cemetery 묘지
be sentenced to death	potter 옹기장, 계획자
사형을 언도받다	potter's field 무연고 묘지

· ·

8 two men were brought in who were paid to tell lies about Jesus
예수님에 대해 거짓을 말하라고 돈을 받은 두 사람이 안으로 들어왔다.

16 he was so guilt-ridden for having him arrested
그는 그(예수님)를 체포하도록 시킨 것 때문에 너무나 죄의식에
시달려서

22 the plot of land where Judas hanged himself
유다가 목을 맨 작은 터

3 it came to be known as "The Field of Blood." 그곳은 "피밭"으로 알려지게
되었다.

제사장과 바리새인이 예수님의
죄명으로 밝힌 것은?

① 매국
② 신성모독
③ 도둑질

Jesus was taken from the High Priest's house to the official residence of Pontius Pilate, the local Roman governor. The Jews had no authority to execute someone who broke Jewish laws, so they had to ask Pilate to handle the matter from here on out. Pilate said to Jesus, "Your own people, the Jews, have handed you over to me. What have you done to deserve death?"

After questioning Jesus, and finding that he had done nothing wrong, Pilate went out to the Jews and said he was going to release him.

But they said, "He has been teaching people doctrines that are against our law and he has been doing this for a long time, starting in the northern province of Galilee."

Since Herod had the right to punish people who broke the law in Galilee, Pilate said, "I find no reason to have this man put to death. Take him to Herod and let him decide what to do!"

official residence 관사, 관저
Pontius Pilate 본디오 빌라도
governor 총독, 통치자
deserve 받기에 족하다,
　　　　…의 가치가 있다

doctrine 교리, 주의, 원칙
province 지방
Galilee 갈릴리
right 권리, 권한

. . . .

7 What have you done to deserve death?
무슨 죽을 만한 짓을 저질렀소?

12 He has been teaching people doctrines that are against our
law 그는 우리의 법에 어긋나는 교리들을 사람들에게 가르쳐왔습니
다.

17 I find no reason to have this man put to death.
나는 이 사람을 사형시킬 만한 이유를 찾지 못하겠소.

Pontius Pilate의 직책은?

① the High Priest
② the local Roman governor
③ the Jewish leader

So, the Jews led Jesus before Herod. He stood in Herod's palace surrounded by Roman soldiers who laughed at him, mocked him, dressed him up in fancy clothes and sent him back to Pilate. Pilate 5 called a meeting with the priests and other Jewish leaders and said, "Neither Herod nor I can find anything that this man has done to deserve the death penalty."

But they shouted, "Yes, he has done bad things! 10 He should be killed!"

Pilate didn't understand why the Jews were so bent on having Jesus killed. He was confused and unsure of what course of action to take. Later, his wife sent a message to 15 him telling him she had had nightmares all night. She advised him to let Jesus go so that he wouldn't be 20 held responsible for the death of a righteous man.

mock 조롱하다
fancy 장식적인, 최고급의
neither ~ nor ··· ~도 ···도 둘 다 아닌
the death penalty 사형
be bent on ···에 열심이다
unsure of ···에 대해 확신이 없는
course 방침, 방향
responsible for ···에 대해 책임이 있는
righteous[ráitʃəs] 의로운

• •

6 Neither Herod nor I can find anything that this man has done to deserve the death penalty.
헤롯왕도 나도 이 사람이 사형 당해 마땅한 죄명을 찾을 수가 없었소.

11 why the Jews were so bent on having Jesus killed
왜 유대인들이 예수를 죽이는데 그토록 열성인지

13 unsure of what course of action to take
어떤 방향의 조치를 취해야 할지 불확실한

18 so that he wouldn't be held responsible for the death of a righteous man
그가 의로운 사람의 죽음에 대해 책임을 지지 않도록

빈 칸에 들어갈 알맞은 말을 본문에서 찾아 쓰시오.

_____ Herod _____
Pilate found Jesus deserved the death penalty.

Just then, Pilate remembered that it was a Jewish custom during the Feast of the Passover to free a prisoner who had been arrested or thrown into prison. By now, there was a sizeable crowd gathered outside Pilate's residence. They were bribed by the priests and Pharisees to shout for Jesus to be killed. Pilate tried to convince the crowd waiting outside to ask for Jesus to be released but they kept shouting,

"Free Barabbas and crucify Jesus!" Barabbas was a notorious criminal who was responsible for the assassination of several Roman soldiers.

Seeing that the crowd was getting out of control, Pilate ordered Jesus to be taken away and whipped. After whipping him, the soldiers made a crown out of thorn branches and put it on his head. They then slapped him in the face, spit at him and said,

"Everyone, hail the King of the Jews!"

The soldiers tortured Jesus so cruelly, but he endured it all with patience and resignation, saying only, "Father, forgive them! They do not know what they are doing!"

free 풀어 주다	get out of …에서 벗어나다
sizeable 상당히 큰, 큼직한	take away 데려가다
residence 주택, 주거, 거주	thorn 가시, 가시 돋친 식물
bribe 뇌물을 주다	spit 침 뱉다
convince 납득시키다	hail 환호성을 올리며 맞이하다,
crucify[krúːsifài] 십자가에 못박다	축하하다
notorious 악명 높은	cruelly 잔인하게
criminal 범죄자	endure 참다, 견디다
assassination	patience 인내
[əsǽsinéiʃ(ə)n] 암살	resignation 체념, 단념

· ·

12 Seeing that the crowd was getting out of control,
군중이 점점 통제 불능상태가 되어 가는 것을 보고는

13 Pilate ordered Jesus to be taken away and whipped 빌라도는
예수님을 데려가 채찍질하라고 명하였다.

14 the soldiers made a crown out of thorn branches and put it
on his head 군인들은 가시 돋친 가지로 왕관을 만들어 그의
머리 위에 씌웠다.

18 he endured it all with patience and resignation,
인내와 체념으로 그 모든 것을 감수하셨다.

What is a Jewish custom
concerning prisoner during
the Feast of the Passover?

① 죄수 중 한 명을 석방
② 형을 감량해줌
③ 죄수 중 한 명을 사형시킴

The people cried out, "Crucify him! Take him away and crucify him!"

"Take him and crucify him yourselves," said Pilate. "I refuse to have anything to do with the
5 death of this innocent man!"

The Pharisees in the crowd shouted to Pilate, "He called himself the son of God and that is against Jewish law. He also called himself the King of the Jews and that is against Roman law. We have no
10 king except Caesar, the Roman Emperor. If you let him go, you are not Caesar's friend. Crucify him! Crucify him!"

When Pilate realized it was no use trying to reason with the crowd, he called for a bowl of water
15 to be brought out to him. He washed his hands in

front of the people and said, "I am not responsible for the blood of this innocent man." Then, he handed Jesus over to the Jews to be crucified. They gathered around him, cursing, kicking and spitting at him as they led him away. All the while, Jesus prayed to God for them.

---

refuse 거부하다, 거절하다
no use ⋯ing ⋯해도 소용없는
reason 이치를 따져 설득하다

call for 요청하다, 요구하다
curse 욕하다, 저주하다
all the while 그 동안 죽, 시종

· ·

4 I refuse to have anything to do with the death of this innocent man! 나는 이 죄 없는 사람의 죽음에 관여하고 싶지 않소.

13 it was no use trying to reason with the crowd, 군중들을 설득하는 것은 소용없는 일이었다.

They gathered around him, cursing, kicking and spitting at him 그들은 그 주위에 몰려들어, 욕을 하고 발길질을 하고 그에게 침을 뱉었다.

All the while, Jesus prayed to God for them. 그러는 동안 내내 예수께서는 그들을 위해 하나님께 기도하셨다.

"He washed his hands in front of the people."의 의미는 무엇인가?

① 무죄한 사람의 죽음에 책임이 없다.
② 재판 후 손을 씻는 것이 당시의 관습이었다.
③ 식사 전이었기 때문에

Chapter Eleven

It was the custom back then to kill people who were sentenced to death by nailing their body onto a big wooden cross. The cross would be placed upright in the ground and the person would be left hanging from it all day and night until they died. It was also a custom to make the condemned person walk to the place of execution carrying the cross in order to increase their torment and disgrace.

Taking up his cross like any common criminal would have to do, our blessed Savior made his way to his death. He was led up a small hill just outside the city gates to a place called Golgotha, which means "skull place" in Hebrew. When they reached the top of the hill, the soldiers hammered large iron nails through his hands and feet to fasten him to the cross. He was placed between two other criminals who were also being crucified that day.

nail 못 박다
upright 똑바로, 수직으로
condemn …에게 선고하다,
　　　　유죄로 판정하다
execution[èksikjúːʃ(ə)n]
　　　　집행, 사형 집행

torment 고통
disgrace 치욕
Golgotha 골고다
skull 해골
Hebrew 히브리어
hammer 망치질하다

· ·

1 It was the custom back then to kill people
who were sentenced to death by nailing
their body onto a big wooden cross.
큰 나무 십자가에 못박아서 사형을 언도 받은
사람을 죽이는 것은 그 당시의 관습이었다.

4 the person would be left hanging from
it all day and night 그 사람은 밤낮으로 거기에
매달려 있게 되는 것이다.

5 It was also a custom to make the
condemned person walk to the place of
execution carrying the cross
형을 선고 받은 사람에게 사형 집행 장소까지 십자가를 지고 가게 하는 것도
또한 (그 당시의) 관습이었다.

9 Taking up his cross like any common criminal would have
to do, our blessed Savior made his way to his death.
보통의 범죄자들이 그래야 했던 것처럼 그의 십자가를 지고서,
성스러운 우리의 구세주는 죽음의 길로 향하셨다.

본문의 내용과 일치하지 <u>않는</u> 것은?

① Golgotha에서 사형이 집행되었다.
② 예수님을 대신해서 제자 중 한 명이
십자가를 지고 갔다.
③ 십자가형을 당한 사람은 모두 세
명이었다.

ANS. 2

All the spectators who passed by derided him and said, "If you really are the son of God, come down from that cross!"

The priests and Pharisees also joined in saying,

5 "He came to save sinners. Let him save himself!"

Even one of the criminals next to him blasphemed and exclaimed, "If you are the Savior, save yourself and us, too!"

There was no one to mourn or take pity on him

10 except one disciple and four women. God blessed these women for their loyal and tender hearts: Mary, the mother of Jesus; his mother's sister; Mary, the wife of Cleopas; and Mary Magdalene. The disciple was John, the one whom Jesus loved the

15 most. When Jesus saw them standing at the foot of the cross, he told his mother that John would be her son from then on, and that he was supposed to take care of her after his death. John, on his part, considered her as his own mother and loved her

20 with all his heart.

spectator 구경꾼
deride[diráid] 조소하다
blaspheme (신성한 것을)
          모독하다
exclaim 외치다, 소리쳐 말하다

mourn 통곡하다
take pity on …을 가엾게 여기다
loyal 충성스러운, 충실한
the wife of Cleopas 세배대의
          아내

. . . .

15 When Jesus saw them standing at the foot of the cross, he told
   his mother that John would be her son from then on,
   예수께서 십자가 밑에 그들이 서있는 것을 보시고, 그의 어머니께
   요한이 지금부터 그녀의 아들이 되어 줄 거라고 말씀하셨다.

17 he was supposed to take care of her after his death
   그는 예수님의 죽음 후에 그녀를 돌보기로 되어
   있었다.

18 John, on his part, considered her
   as his own mother
   요한의 편에서도 그녀를 그의
   친어머니처럼 생각했다.

십자가형을 구경하는 군중들의
공통적인 반응은?

① sad
② mocking
③ pitiful

From about noon until three o'clock, darkness covered the Earth. Then Jesus cried out in a loud voice, "My God, my God, why have you abandoned me?" The soldiers who were standing nearby, put 5 some vinegar on a sponge, tied it to a long stick and held it up to his mouth.

He drank a little and then said, "It is finished! Father, into your hands I commend my spirit!" Then he died.

10 Suddenly, there was a mighty earthquake and the great wall of the temple cracked, rocks split open and dead men rose from their graves. The soldiers who were guarding Jesus said to one another, "Surely this man was the son of God!" The 15 crowd who had been watching from a distance, beat their breasts and fled in fear and remorse.

Since the next day was the Sabbath, the Jewish leaders wanted the bodies removed from the crosses as soon as possible. So, they went to Pilate and 20 received permission for this. Soldiers came and broke the legs of the two criminals who were crucified along with Jesus in order to hasten their imminent deaths. But when they came to Jesus and saw that he was already dead, they only pierced his side near his heart with a lance. Out of the wound flowed blood and water.

abandon 버리다	breast 가슴, 흉부
vinegar 식초	hasten 재촉하다
hold up 위로 치켜들다, 올리다	imminent 임박한
commend 맡기다, 위탁하다	pierce 찌르다
mighty 강력한	lance[læns] 창
crack 금이 가다	wound 상처
split 쪼개지다	flow 흐르다

· ·

8 Father, into your hands I commend my spirit!
아버지여, 당신의 손에 제 영혼을 맡기나이다!

14 The crowd who had been watching from a distance, beat their breasts and fled in fear and remorse. 멀리서 지켜보았던 군중들은 가슴을 치며 두려움과 죄책감에 사로잡혀 도망을 쳤다.

17 Since the next day was the Sabbath, the Jewish leaders wanted the bodies removed from the crosses as soon as possible. 다음 날이 안식일이었으므로, 유대인 지도자들은 가능한 빨리 시체들을 십자가에서 치우기를 원했다.

3 Out of the wound flowed blood and water. 상처로부터 피와 물이 흘러나왔다.

십자가형이 집행된 후 일어난 일이 아닌 것은?

① 큰 지진이 일어남
② 죽은 자들이 살아남
③ 홍수가 일어남

In Jerusalem, there was an upright man named Joseph of Arimathea, who happened to be a Jewish leader. He was also a secret follower of Jesus, so he courageously went to Pilate and requested that he be given the body. Pilate agreed, and then he and Nicodemus, another secret follower of Jesus, rolled it in some burial spices and linen cloth as was the custom in those days. They brought Jesus's body to a garden near the place of the crucifixion and placed it in a new tomb, which had recently been hewn out of a rock. Then they rolled a large, heavy stone in front of the entrance and left Mary Magdalene and the other Mary sitting there, watching it.

The priests and Pharisees remembered that Jesus had told his disciples that he would come to life again on the third day after his death. So, they went to Pilate and asked him to place a guard at the tomb night and day in case his disciples tried to come and steal the body. They could then tell everyone that Jesus had risen from the dead just as he said and that would make him more popular than ever. Pilate agreed with their plan and posted a twenty-four-hour watch at the entrance to the tomb. And so it remained sealed and guarded until the third day, which was Sunday.

upright 바른, 정직한, 고결한	linen cloth 모시천, 아마포천,
Joseph of Arimathea	crucifixion [kru:sifíkʃ(ə)n]
아리마대 요셉	십자가에 못박힘
follower 추종자	hew [hju:] 자르다
courageously 대담하게	(hew-hewed-hewed or hewn)
request 요청하다	come to life 살아나다
Nicodemus 니고데모	in case …의 경우에 대비하여
roll …을 감싸다, 싸다, 둘러싸다	post (병사 등을) 배치하다
spice 향료, 향신료	seal 밀폐하다

· ·

4 (he) requested that he be given the body
그에게 예수님의 시체를 달라고 요청했다.

6 rolled it in some burial spices and linen cloth as was the custom in those days 그 당시의 관습대로 시체에 향신료를 발라 모시천에 쌌다.

18 in case his disciples tried to come and steal the body
그의 제자들이 와서 시체를 훔치려 할 것에 대비하여

20 Jesus had risen from the dead just as he said
예수께서 말씀하신 대로 죽음에서 살아나셨다.

22 (Pilate) posted a twenty-four-hour watch at the entrance to the tomb
무덤 입구에 24시간 경비병을 배치했다.

제사장들과 바리새인들이 예수님의 무덤을 봉하고 경비병을 둔 이유를 간단히 우리말로 설명하시오.

When dawn appeared in the sky that morning, Mary Magdalene, the other Mary and some other women came walking to the tomb with more spices and oils to anoint Jesus's body. They knew that there
5 was a large stone blocking the entrance and they said to one another, "How will we be able to move that stone all by ourselves?" Just then, the earth shook and an angel came down from heaven, rolled back the stone and sat on it. His face was as
10 dazzling as lightning and his clothes were whiter than snow. Seeing this, the guards who were watching the tomb fainted with fear and looked as if they were dead.

dawn 새벽	by oneself 혼자서, 혼자 힘으로
anoint[ənɔ́int] 기름을 바르다	dazzling 눈부신, 찬란한
block 막다	faint 기절할 듯한, 어질어질한
entrance 입구, 출구	as if 마치 …인 것처럼

· ·

8 rolled back the stone 바위를 원래대로 굴렸다.

9 His face was as dazzling as lightning
   그의 얼굴은 번개처럼 눈부시게 빛이 났다.

11 Seeing this, the guards who were watching the tomb fainted
   with fear and looked as if they were dead.
                이것을 보고, 무덤을 지키던 경비병들이 두려운 나머지
                기절을 해 마치 죽은 사람처럼 보였다.

Who moved the stone
blocking the entrance?

① the guards
② Mary Magdalene
③ an angel

ANS.3

By the time the women reached the tomb, they saw that the stone had been rolled away. They were astonished and ran to tell Peter and John, who were also on their way to the tomb. They screamed,
5 "Someone has taken away our Lord and we don't know where his body is!" Peter and John immediately raced to the tomb, but since John was younger and faster, he arrived there first. He stooped down to look inside and saw the linen cloth
10 in which Jesus's body had been wrapped. Then Peter came up and went inside the tomb and saw the

linen cloths neatly folded up in one place and a separate piece of cloth that had been tied around the head in another place. After this, they went back to Jerusalem together to tell the rest of the disciples.

by the time …할 즈음에	wrap 싸다, 포장하다
astonished 놀란	neatly 단정하게
scream 비명을 지르다	fold up 반듯이 접다
stoop down 구부리다, 웅크리다	separate 별개의

· ·

1 By the time the women reached the tomb,
  그 여자들이 무덤에 도착했을 무렵에
3 Peter and John, who were also on their way to the tomb
  베드로와 요한에게 말하려고 달려갔는데, 그들도 또한 무덤으로 오고 있는 길이었다.
7 since John was younger and faster,
  요한이 더 젊고 빨랐으므로
9 saw the linen cloth in which Jesus's body had been wrapped 예수님의 시체를 감싸두었던
  모시천을 보았다.

예수님의 시신이 사라진 것을 보고 여인들은 무슨 생각을 했는가?

① 예수님이 부활하셨다.
② 누군가가 예수님의 시신을 훔쳐갔다.
③ 누군가가 예수님의 시신을 화장했다.

Mary Magdalene stayed outside the tomb weeping. A little while later, she decided to go into the tomb herself. There she saw two angels, clothed in white, sitting where Jesus's body had lain. They
5 said to her, "Woman, why are you crying?"

She answered, "Because someone has taken away my Lord and I don't know where he is." Then she turned around to leave and saw Jesus standing there, but she didn't recognize him at first.

10 "Woman," he said to her, "why are you crying? Who are you looking for?"

She thought he must be the gardener and so she answered, "Sir! If you have taken my Lord's body from this tomb, tell me where you have put him
15 and I will take him away."

Jesus said her name, "Mary," and then she realized it was our Savior.

She cried out, "Lord!" and went to hug him but he stopped her saying, "Don't touch me. I haven't
20 yet ascended to my Father! Go back to my disciples and tell them what you have seen."

weep 울다
a little while later 잠시 후에
take away 가져가다, 데려가다
turn around 뒤를 돌다

recognize 알아보다, 식별하다
gardener 정원사
realize 깨닫다
ascend 올라가다

· ·

3 There she saw two angels, clothed in white, sitting where
Jesus's body had lain. 그녀는 거기서 하얀 옷을 입은 두 명의
천사가 예수님의 시체가 놓여있었던 곳에 앉아 있는 것을 보았다.

19 he stopped her saying, "Don't touch me."
그는 "나를 만지지 말라"라고 말씀하시며 그녀를
저지하셨다.

Mary는 처음에 살아나신 예수님을
누구라고 생각했는가?

① an angel
② the guard
③ the gardener

She ran as fast as her legs could carry her back to the upper room, where Jesus had eaten the Last Supper with his disciples, and she told them all that had happened. Among the disciples were some of 5 the other women who had first gone to the tomb with Mary Magdalene. They too told the disciples that they had seen two angels in shining clothes. At first, they were frozen with fear, but the angels told them not to be afraid and that Jesus had risen from 10 the dead. They also saw the Lord near the tomb and had knelt at his feet and worshipped him. The disciples didn't believe the women because it all sounded too preposterous.

The soldiers who had been guarding the tomb 15 finally recovered from their shock and bolted off to inform the priests and Pharisees of everything they had seen. They were induced to keep silent about what had actually happened with a financial incentive. Instead, they were supposed to spread a 20 rumor that Jesus's disciples had come in the middle of the night and stolen his body.

frozen 얼어붙은	induce 타일러서 …시키다,
worship 참배하다, 숭배하다	설득하다
preposterous [pripást(ə)rəs]	financial 재정상의, 금융상의
터무니없는, 비상식적인	incentive 자극, 유인, 동기
bolt 뛰어나가다, 도망치다	in the middle of …한 가운데

······························

1 She ran as fast as her legs could carry her back to the upper
room, where Jesus had eaten the Last Supper with his disciples,
그녀는 가능한 빨리 그 이층 방으로 달려갔는데, 그곳은 예수님이 제자들과
최후의 만찬을 드셨던 곳이었다.

4 Among the disciples were some of the other women who had
first gone to the tomb with Mary Magdalene.
막달라 마리아와 함께 맨 처음 무덤으로 갔던 다른 여자들도 제자들과 함께
있었다.

7 At first, they were frozen with fear,
처음에 그들은 두려움으로 얼어붙었다.

15 recovered from their shock and bolted off to inform the priests
and Pharisees of everything they had seen
충격에서 벗어나서 제사장들과 바리새인들에게 그들이 목격한 모든 것을
알리고자 급히 달려나갔다.

17 They were induced to keep silent about what had actually
happened with a financial incentive.
그들은 금전적인 보상을 받고 실제로 일어났던 일들에
대해 침묵하기로 하였다.

19 Instead, they were supposed to spread
a rumor 대신에 그들은 소문을 퍼뜨리기로
되어있었다.

> How did the disciples feel
> when they heard from the
> women that Jesus had risen
> from the dead?
>
> ① 두려움　　② 기쁨　　③ 걱정스러움

It just so happened that Simon and Cleopas, two followers of Jesus, were traveling on foot that same day to a small town called Emmaus, which was not far from Jerusalem. As they were walking along and
5 discussing the events of the last few days, a stranger came and joined them on the road. This stranger interpreted for them the parts of the Bible that pertained to Jesus. The two men were highly impressed at his remarkable eloquence and so they
10 urged him to stay with them in Emmaus as it was getting late. When they all three sat down to eat supper, the stranger took some bread, blessed it, and broke it as Jesus had done at the Last Supper. The two men looked at him in amazement and saw
15 that his face had changed right before their eyes! It was the Lord! As they sat staring at him, he disappeared.

It just so happened
that... 우연히 …하다
Emmaus 엠마오
interpret
        설명하다, 해석하다
pertain to 관계하다
highly 매우
impress 감동시키다
remarkable 주목할 만한,
        놀랄 만한, 뛰어난
eloquence [éləkwəns]
        능변, 웅변
urge 간청하다, 촉구하다
amazement 경악

· ·

6 This stranger interpreted for them the parts of the Bible that
  pertained to Jesus.
  이 낯선 사람은 예수님과 관련된 성경의 부분들을 그들에게 해석해 주었다.

8 The two men were highly impressed at his remarkable
  eloquence 그 두 사람은 그의 놀라운 말솜씨에 매우 감명을 받았다.

13 as Jesus had done at the Last Supper
   예수께서 최후의 만찬에서 그러셨던 것처럼

16 As they sat staring at him,
   그들이 그 낯선 사람을 바라보며 앉아 있었을 때

Emmaus로 가는 Simon과
Cleopas에게 나타나 성경을 설명
해 준 사람은 누구인가?

At once, they got up and returned to Jerusalem to tell the disciples they had seen the Lord. While they were speaking, Jesus himself suddenly stood in their midst and said, "Peace be with you!" Everyone 5 thought they were seeing a ghost and were overcome with fright. Then Jesus showed them his hands and feet and told them to touch him. He even ate a piece of fish and some bread on the table.

At that time, Thomas, one of the disciples, was 10 not there, and when the others told him, "We have seen the Lord!" he said stubbornly, "I will not believe until I see the marks of the nails in his hands and put my hand into the wound in his side!" Just then, even though all the doors were locked, 15 Jesus again appeared in the room and said, "Peace with you!" Then he said to Thomas, "Come here and look at my hands and put your own hand into the 20 hole in my side. Do not persist in your unbelief but believe!"

Thomas replied, "My Lord and my God!"

And Jesus said to him, "Thomas, you have believed because you have seen me. Blessed are those who have never seen me and still believe!"

---

midst 한복판, 가운데	stubbornly 고집스럽게, 완강하게
be overcome with …로 압도되다	mark 표시
fright 공포, 경악	persist in …을 고집하다, 주장하다
Thomas 도마	unbelief 불신

••••••••••••••••••••••••••••

4 Peace be with you! 너희에게 평안이 있으라!

5 (they) were overcome with fright (그들은) 공포에 사로잡혀 있었다.

13 put my hand into the wound in his side 옆구리에 있는 상처에 손을 넣어보다.

14 even though all the doors were locked, 모든 문이 잠겨 있었는데도

20 Do not persist in your unbelief but believe! 불신을 고집하지 말고 믿음을 가져라!

3 Blessed are those who have never seen me and still believe! 나를 보지 않고도 믿는 자들은 축복을 받을 것이다!

마지막까지 예수님의 부활을 믿지 <u>않은</u> 제자는?

① Peter
② Thomas
③ John

ANS. 2

Several weeks later, Jesus was seen by five hundred of his followers at one time. He stayed with them for about forty days, preparing them to be his apostles. Their mission would be to go out
5 into the whole world and proclaim the good news. After he had told them everything they needed to know, he led them out to Bethany, blessed them and ascended to heaven, taking his seat at the right hand of God. While the disciples were standing
10 there looking up into the sky, two angels dressed in white appeared and told them that just as they had seen Jesus go up to heaven, he would come back down one day.

at one time 동시에, 한번에,
prepare 준비시키다
apostle [əpásl] 사도, 제자

mission 임무, 사명
proclaim 선포하다
right hand 우측, 오른쪽

....

1 Jesus was seen by five hundred of his followers at one time
동시에 오백 명의 추종자들에게 예수께서 나타나셨다.

3 preparing them to be his apostles
그들을 그의 사도로 준비시키시면서

4 Their mission would be to go out into the whole world and
proclaim the good news.
그들의 사명은 전세계로 나가 복음을 선포하는 것이었다.

8 ascended to heaven, taking his seat at the right hand of God
하늘로 올라가신 후 하나님의 오른편에 앉으셨다.

11 just as they had seen Jesus go up to heaven, he would come
back down one day 예수께서 하늘로 올라가는 것을 본 것처럼 언젠가
그가 다시 오실 것이다.

How long did Jesus stay with
his disciples after rising from
the dead? Write in English.

ANS. (He stayed with them)
For about forty days.

The disciples returned to Jerusalem filled with joy and began to teach people as Jesus had ordered them to. They chose a new disciple named Matthias to replace Judas, the disciple who betrayed Jesus. 5 With power and authority, they went out to all countries, telling people about Jesus's life, death and resurrection. They taught the lessons that Jesus had taught them, baptized people in Jesus's name, healed the sick, made the blind see and the deaf hear. Once 10 Peter was arrested and thrown into jail, but an angel came during the night and helped him to escape.

Remember, dear readers, that the Christian religion comes from Jesus. Christianity teaches us to do good always, even to those who hurt us. 15 Christianity tells us to love our neighbors as ourselves and to do to others what we would like them to do to us. It is Christian to be tolerant, docile, clement and self-effacing, never boasting about our virtue to others. It is Christian to show 20 that we love God by being unassuming and by trying to do what is right at all times and in all circumstances. If we do this and remember the life and lessons of our Savior, Jesus Christ, we can believe that God will forgive our sins and take us to heaven when we die to be happy with Him forever.

Matthias 맛디아
baptize 세례를 주다
escape 탈출하다
Christian 그리스도교의, 기독교의
Christianity 그리스도교, 기독교
tolerant 관대한, 아량 있는
docile[dóusail] 유순한,
　　　　가르치기 쉬운

clement 관대한, 온순한
self-effacing 표면에 나서지 않는
boast 자랑하다
virtue 미덕
unassuming 주제넘지 않는,
　　　　겸손한
at all times 항상
circumstance 상황

. . . .

12 the Christian religion comes from Jesus
기독교는 예수님께로서 비롯되었다.

15 to love our neighbors as ourselves and to do to others what we
would like them to do to us 이웃을 우리 자신처럼 사랑하고 우리가
대우받고 싶은 대로 다른 사람들을 대우하라.

17 It is Christian to be tolerant, docile, clement and self-
effacing, never boasting about our virtue to others.
아량 있고, 유순하며, 관대하고, 나서지 않으며, 자신의
미덕을 다른 사람들에게 결코 자랑하지 않는 것이
기독교적인 것이다.

예수님이 승천하신 후 제자들의
모습으로 적절치 않은 것은?

① 모두 뿔뿔이 흩어졌다.
② 담대하게 예수님의 가르침을 전했다.
③ 병자들을 고쳤다.

Comprehension
Checkup III

I. Judas가 예수님을 체포하러 왔을 때, 사람들이 보인 반응을 서로 연결하시오.

① 예수님　　　　　　　　ⓐ cut off the right ear of one of the high priests' servant

② Peter　　　　　　　　ⓑ surrendered himself to the soldiers

③ other disciples　　　　ⓒ deserted him and ran off into the darkness

2. 본문을 다시 살펴보면서 예수님에 관한 재판이 진행되었던 장소들을 찾아 빈 칸을 채우시오.

> ＿＿＿＿＿＿＿＿＿ ⇒ the official residence of Pontius Pilate ⇒ ＿＿＿＿＿＿＿ ⇒ the official residence of Pontius Pilate

3. 예수님을 팔아 넘긴 후 Judas가 취한 행동이 <u>아닌</u> 것은?

① 자살을 함　　　　　　　② 예수를 찾아가 회개함

③ 제사장들에게 받은 은 삼십 냥을 다시 돌려줌

4. 당시 유대인들의 사형제도에 대한 설명으로 올바른 것은?

① 십자가에 못박았다.

② 교수형에 처했다.

③ 화형에 처했다.

5. Why did Pilate hand Jesus over to the Jews to be crucified?

① 성난 군중들을 설득하는 것이 소용없음을 깨달았기 때문에
② 십자가형을 당할 만한 죄명을 발견했기 때문에
③ Herod 왕의 명을 받아서

6. 다음의 나열된 인물들의 공통점은 무엇인지 빈 칸을 채우시오.

> Peter, Matthias, John, Simon, Judas, James
> They are all _____ .

7. 빈 칸에 들어갈 알맞은 말은?

> Christianity tells us to love _____ as
> ourselves and to do to them what we would like
> them to do to us.

① our family   ② the poor   ③ our neighbors

8. 다음의 this가 가르키는 것이 무엇인지 영어로 쓰시오.

> Jesus died on this. This was placed upright in the
> ground and criminals were left hanging from this.
> This is the symbol of Christianity.

정답은 p.128에

Answers

Comprehension Checkup

Checkup I (40~41쪽)

1. ③
2. ③
3. Bethlehem, Egypt, Nazareth
4. ②
5. ③
6. ①-a, ②-c, ③-b
7. ②
8. ①
9. ①

Checkup II (80~81쪽)

1. You must love God with all your heart.
2. ①
3. ①
4. ②
5. ②
6. ①
7. ③
8. ①

Checkup III (126~127쪽)

1. ①-b, ②-a, ③-c
2. Caiaphas's house, Herod's palace
3. ②
4. ①
5. ①
6. disciples
7. ③
8. cross

(((Songs)))

Song 1

A baby, Jesus was born as a son of God in Bethlehem to show everyone love and peace. Some shepherds came and worshiped him. The wise men gave him gold, incense, and myrrh. They all proclaimed together, "God bless this child!"

Song 2

Jesus loves children, humble and innocent. Jesus loves sinners regretting what they did. Jesus loves disciples always following him. Jesus loves his neighbors as himself. We should love each other as Jesus did.

Song 3

Feed the hungry, cure the sick, raise the dead. These are the things Jesus was doing on earth. But some people hated him and tried to kill him. They crucified him. How painful it was! His disciples denied and deserted him. How sad he was!

Word List

다음은 이 책에 나오는 단어를 수록한 것입니다.
＊표는 교육부 고시 교육과정에서 제시하는 기본 어휘입니다.

abandon 버리다

accompany 함께 다니다

accomplish 성취하다, 이루다

adequate 어울리는, 적당한

affair＊ 일, 관심사, 사건

afflict 괴롭히다

amend 개정하다, 수정하다

anguish 고통, 괴로움, 번민

animosity 적대감

apologize 사과하다

appearance 외관, 겉모양

arrest＊ 체포하다

arrogant 거만한, 오만한

ascend 올라가다

ashamed＊ 부끄러워하는

assemble 모으다, 조립하다

assure 확실하게 하다

astonish 놀라게 하다

attach＊ 붙이다

attack＊ 공격하다

attempt＊ 시도하다

authority＊ 권한, 권위

betray 배신하다, 배반하다

bitter 쓴, 모진

boast＊ 자랑하다

burial 매장

burst 파열하다, 폭발하다

cancel＊ 취소하다

cathedral 성당

celebrate＊ 경축하다, 축하하다

celestial 천상의, 하늘의

cemetery 묘지

charity* 자애, 자비

circumstance 상황, 환경

comfort 위로하다

command* 명령하다

comment* 주석, 논평

commit* 범하다, 저지르다

compassion 불쌍히 여김, 동정

conceive 마음에 품다, 생각하다

concern* 관계하다;
　　　　　관계, 관심, 염려

condemn 비난하다,
　　　　　판결을 내리다

confidence 자신감, 확신

consequence 결과

contain* 포함하다

contribute* 기부하다

convince 납득시키다, 확신시키다

criminal 범죄자

crisis* 위기

cure* 치료하다

curse 저주하다

custom* 관습, 풍습

dawn* 새벽

deaf* 귀먹은

decent 예의 바른, 품위 있는

deny* 부인하다

descend* 내려가다

desert* 버리다

deserve …을 받을 가치가 있다

despair 절망, 자포자기

desperate 자포자기의

destitute 빈곤한, 결핍한

disappear 사라지다

disappoint 실망시키다

disciple 제자

discuss* 토론하다

disease* 질병

disgrace 창피, 불명예

dispatch 급송하다

distress 비탄, 고통

duty* 의무

eloquence 웅변, 능변

endure 참다, 인내하다

escape* 탈출하다

essential 필수적인

esteem 존경하다, 존중하다

eternal 영원한
evil* 사악한
exclaim 외치다
excuse* 용서하다, 변명하다
execution 실행, 처형
extraordinary 이상한,
보통이 아닌

faint* 기절하다
faith* 믿음
fasten* 고정시키다
feed* 먹을 것을 주다
financial* 재정상의, 재무의
flee 도망치다
force* 억지로 …시키다
frozen 언, 차가운
frustrate 실망시키다, 좌절시키다
fulfillment 성취, 달성
furious 격분한

generous* 관대한
genuine* 진짜의
gracious 호의적인, 친절한

grateful* 감사하고 있는
greedy 욕심 많은, 탐욕스러운
grief 슬픔
guilty* 유죄의, 죄를 범한

hail 환호하며 맞이하다
hammer* 망치로 치다,
(못 따위를) 쳐서 박다
hang* 매달다, 걸다, 목매다
hardly* 거의 …않다
harm* 손해, 손상; 해치다,
손상하다
hasten 서두르다
heal 치유하다
holy* 거룩한
horrid 무서운
huge* 거대한, 막대한
humble 천한, 겸손한

imminent 절박한, 급박한
impress* 인상지우다
incense 향
increase* 증가하다

induce 꾀다, 권유하다

infant 유아

inform* 알리다

inhabitant 거주자, 주민

inheritance 유산

innocent 순진한, 죄가 없는

insight 통찰력

insist* 주장하다, 고집하다

instruction* 교수, 교훈, 가르침

interpret 해석하다, 통역을 하다

invoke 기원하다, 호소하다

jealous 시기하는, 질투하는

judge* 재판관; 판단하다

lay* 눕히다, 두다

lick* 핥다

lie* 눕다, 놓여있다

limit* 제한하다

livestock 가축

loaf 덩어리

local* 공간의, 지방의

loyal 충성스러운, 성실한

luxury 사치(품), 호사

malicious 악의 있는

mankind 인류

master* 주인; 숙달하다

meanwhile 그 동안, 그 사이에

mental* 정신적인

merciful 자비로운

mighty 강력한, 위대한

military* 군의, 군대의

miserable 비참한

mission 임무, 전도

mob 군중, 폭도의 떼

mock 조롱하다

moral* 도덕의; 교훈

mount 오르다, 타다

mourn 슬퍼하다, 한탄하다

mysterious 신비로운

neglect 게을리 하다; 태만, 부주의

nevertheless 그럼에도 불구하고,
그렇지만

normal* 정상의, 표준의

notorious 악명 높은

object* 반대하다, 항의하다
occasion* 경우, 기회, 이유
occupation* 직업
offend* 성나게 하다,
　　　　　기분을 상하게 하다
official* 공무의, 공식의, 공무원
opposite* 반대의
oppressive 압박하는
overcome* 극복하다
owe* 빚지다, 은혜를 입다

pain* 고통
parable 우화
participate 참여하다
patience 인내
perform* 실행하다, 이행하다
perilous 위험한, 모험적인
permission 허가, 면허
persist 고집하다, 주장하다
persuade* 설득하다, 납득시키다
pertain 속하다, 관계하다

pierce 꿰뚫다, 관통하다
pity* 불쌍히 여김, 동정
plead 변호하다
possess* 소유하다
preach 전도하다, 설교하다
prepare* 준비하다
present* 선사하다, 주다
prevent 막다
priest* 성직자, 목사
proclaim 포고하다, 선언하다
profess 공언하다, 고백하다
prominent 눈에 띄는, 저명한
protect* 보호하다
protest* 항의하다, 항변하다
punish* 벌하다, 응징하다

quarrelsome 싸우기를 좋아하는

rank* 열, 계급, 지위
react* 반응하다
recall 회상하다
recognize* 인식하다, 알아보다
recover* 되찾다, 회복하다

refuge 피난, 피난처
release 풀어놓다, 석방하다
remarkable 주목할 만한, 현저한
replace* 대신하다
reply* 대답하다
request* 구하다, 원하다
require* 요구하다, 필요로 하다
residence 주거, 주택, 거주
resignation 사직, 사임
resolve 용해하다, 결의하다
respond 응답하다, 대답하다
responsible* 책임 있는
reveal* 드러내다, 폭로하다
rude* 무례한

sacred 신성한
scholar 학자
scream 소리치다, 비명을 지르다
seal 봉하다, 밀폐하다
search* 찾다, 탐색하다
seize 붙잡다, 꽉 쥐다
sentence* 형을 선고하다
separate* 분리하다
serious* 진지한, 중대한
settle 놓다, 자리잡게 하다

severe* 엄한, 엄격한
share* 몫, 분배하다, 나누다
shelter 피난 장소, 오두막, 숙소
signal* 신호하다, 눈짓하다
similar* 유사한
sincere* 성실한, 진실한
skull 두개골, 머리
slaughter 살해하다
slumber 잠
spirit 정신, 마음, 영혼
spit 침을 뱉다
splendid 빛나는, 화려한
split* 쪼개다, 찢다
spot* 반점, 장소
spread* 펴다, 펼치다
starve 굶주리다, 배고프다
stretch* 뻗치다, 늘이다
struggle* 노력하다, 분투하다
stumble 넘어지다, 비틀거리다
suicide 자살
superior* 보다 위의, 보다 높은
surrender 내어주다, 넘겨주다
surround* 둘러싸다
survive* 생존하다, 살아남다
swear* 맹세하다

tend* 돌보다
threaten 위협하다
tolerant 관대한, 아량 있는
transform 변형시키다, 바꾸다

upright 수직의, 곧은
upset* 뒤집어엎다, 당황케 하다,
urge 재촉하다, 주장하다

violent* 폭력적인
virtue* 미덕

weep 울다
whip 채찍질하다
wicked* 사악한
widow 과부
withhold 보류하다, 억누르다
witness 목격하다
worship 숭배하다, 경배하다
worthy 훌륭한, 가치 있는
wound 부상, 상처; 상처를 입히다
wrap* 감싸다, 싸다

Yellow Series · Pink Series

1,200단어 수준(Yellow Series),
2,800단어 수준(Pink Series)으로 분류하여 자신의
실력에 맞춰 골라 읽는 영어 소설 / 전 30권

Yellow Series

Pink Series

사전 없이 읽는

세계 명작
영어 학습 문고

난이도에 따라 주니어편(♣), 초급편(★), 중급편(★★),
고급편(★★★)으로 나눈 문고의 스테디 셀러 / 전 80권

고급편(★★★)

주니어편(♣)

영한 대역 문고

학문적 깊이와 흥미를 만족시킬 수 있는 작품들만을 엄선해 원문과 함께
대역을 실어 준 세계 명작 고급편 / 전 100권

세계 명작 Spring Series 목록

영어로 읽는
세계 명작 스프링 시리즈

2000년 1월 5일 초판발행
2010년 6월 5일 인   쇄
2010년 6월 10일 중쇄발행

발행인 : 민 선 식

YBM Si-sa

서울특별시 종로구 종로 2가 55-1
TEL (02) 2000-0515
FAX (02) 2271-0172

등록일자 : 1964년 3월 28일
등록번호 : 제 1-214호

인터넷 홈페이지 : http://www.ybmbooks.com